That Young Hood Love 2

TN Jones

Acknowledgments

First, thanks must go out to the Higher Being for providing me with a sound body and mind in addition to having the natural talent of writing and blessing me with the ability to tap into such an amazing part of life. Second, thanks most definitely go out to my Princess. Third, Tyanna Coston, Tyanna Presents, and Shanice B. Fourth, to my supporters who have been rocking with me from day one and to new readers for giving me a chance.

Truth be told, I wouldn't have made it this far without anyone. I truly thank everyone for rocking with me. Muah! Y'all make this writing journey enjoyable. I would like to thank everyone from the bottom of my heart for always rocking with the novelist kid from Alabama no matter what I drop. Y'all have once again trusted me to provide y'all with quality entertainment. I hope y'all enjoy, my loves!

Chapter 1

Marlon

Sunday, May 6th

Big Juke and Big Nuke were well-known, powerful, dope boys and cousins. They sold illegal drugs from heroin to pills. One day, they were peddling nickel and dime bags of weed, and the next, they were untouchable. Not a soul knew how in the hell they rose to power at such a young age—just fifteen years old. Now, at the tender age of 22, these motherfuckers ran Tuscaloosa and several other areas surrounding the city.

I was surprised that my family and I were still alive honestly. Those niggas didn't play the radio when it came down to their family members. They heavily believed in family and loyalty. Big Juke and Big Nuke were like me and my family when it came down to Myia, Trandall, Sasha, and me. They would lay down their lives about their own as we would about ours.

Shit went to the left the moment Big Juke spotted Trandall at a ducked off service station. Willingly getting into the van, Trandall shook his head. Afterwards, we pulled into Quinn's driveway. Big Juke and I went back and forth about not needing to involve my kid and her mother. Of course, he snatched them up anyway. At least, the motherfucker had the decency to grab Marlia's tablet and *Frozen*-themed headphones. I applauded him for that. Yet, he was still on my shit list.

My thoughts were all over the place the moment my child was placed in my arms. She didn't look scared or worried. She happily called my name before planting several small kisses on my nose. Once I alienated her from our current situation, I began to think about how in the fuck I was going to get my fam out of a situation they had no business being in. I didn't want anything happening to my daughter because of some shit I had gotten myself into—fucking with some thot bitches who were trying to set me up.

My thoughts ceased the moment I realized that Big Juke was pulling into Ms. Suelle's driveway.

"What in the fuck are we doing here?" I asked in a not so pleasant voice.

They didn't respond; they just exited the van quickly.

"What in the fuck?" Trandall spat as he wiggled in the chair he was tied to.

"One thing I know, they better not do a damn thing to either of them. I'mma get us out of this jam," I told him as I didn't tear my eyes away from the front door.

I was on pins and needles as I sweated to see my sister and Sasha come out the house running to get away, but the look of sadness and disappointment was plastered across my face as I watched Big Juke and Big Nuke bring them out.

"Fuck!" Trandall said as I sighed heavily and shook my head.

If a nigga didn't want to bust that motherfucker Big Nuke in the face before he pulled up at Quinn's crib, I sure as hell did the second he knocked Sasha out before carefully placing her inside the van.

"Motherfucka, you ain't had to do all that," I nastily snarled before he closed the sliding door.

As Big Nuke ran back inside of the house, Big Juke hopped in the driver's seat of the old school van. My mind wondered why Big Nuke went back inside of the house. I didn't have to wonder for long as he came waltzed towards the van.

The moment he sat in the passenger seat, I said, "Let my motherfuckin' fam go, Big Nuke! Yo' issue is wit' me, not them ... especially not my child!"

"Like I told yo' ass before, we gonna show you how things are done the Tuscaloosa-way. I got some wonderful things in store fo' yo' fam like you had in store fo' mine," Big Juke spat as Big Nuke place the gearshift in reverse.

Never in a million years would I have thought that those two bitches from Huntingdon College would be my demise. Not understanding how in the fuck I got them pregnant to begin with had a nigga's head hurting like fuck. I used condoms every time I smashed them. I wasn't looking for either of them to be my woman. I was just seeking a fun time with two freaky bitches.

As the van skirted away from Ms. Suelle's home, I made eye contact with each of my family members. The look in Myia's eyes showed that she was scared and worried. Trandall had a blank facial expression as he glared at me, and Sasha was finally coming too. When she realized that she was in the back of a van, she didn't look my way as she asked the Big's where they were taking us. They didn't respond, further pissing Sasha off.

Seeing that she wasn't getting anywhere with the ruthless pair, Sasha placed her eyes on Marlia, whom was watching YouTube. I had to push the earbuds into her small ears as they slid out for the tenth time. I didn't bother to look at Quinn; she was knocked out from a blow that Big Juke sent to her face. Honestly, I didn't give a damn about her. She got what she deserved for being a bitch beyond return.

The ride to Tuscaloosa was long, yet, it gave me a chance to figure out how I was going to get my family out of the jam we were placed in. It wasn't like I was lying about not seeing the message those broads sent me. If I would've seen the message, I would've handled my business all the while letting them know that I highly doubted that I got them pregnant.

"Aye, lil' sexy chocolate, you are beautiful. When all this shit blows over ... *if* it blows over, how 'bout I take you on a date?" Big Nuke questioned Sasha seriously.

"Nawl, bruh, she good," I spat as I placed my eyes on the tall, athletic, light-skinned nigga who stood around six-foot and some inches.

Chuckling, he replied, "The best thing you can do is shut the fuck up an' learn how to be a man. Stop takin' care of *one* child an' take care of three."

Getting angry, I snarled, "Like I motherfuckin' said before, I ain't get nobody pregnant other than the bitch who's knocked out. Mona an' Janelle are lyin'. They probably don't know who knocked them up. Shid, I wasn't the only one they were fuckin'. I just had common sense to use a fuckin' rubber ... every single damn time. If only you knew the type of shit they were doin' in Da Gump."

"You better watch yo' tone, nigga," Big Juke spat as he turned around, glaring into my face with his squinty, cold, hazel-green, eyes.

"Nawl, y'all need to watch y'all's tone. Come grabbin' up my folks on some humbug shit."

In a flash, all I saw were birds and stars as my eyelids closed.

***

"Why in the fuck are we here?" Quinn asked nastily while looking at Big Juke.

"Because yo' fuck-ass baby daddy ain't takin' care of his damn kids," Mona spat as she waltzed through the door.

"What kids?" Quinn inquired while looking at me.

"Mine and my cousin Janelle's son," Mona voiced as she walked slowly towards the center of the living room.

"Cousin Juke?" Mona said.

"Yeah?" he replied as he glared at his whorish cousin who had the nerve to be dressed in clothing that didn't show her off assets.

"I think we need to show Marlon what it's like to raise a child on his own," she replied with an evil smile on her face as she stared at Quinn.

Being the asshole that I was, I held a huge grin as I said, "Shid, be my fuckin' guest. She be on some mo' shit anyway."

There wasn't a thing that anyone in the room could say, not even Quinn. At that particular moment, she knew that I didn't give a damn about her. She knew that I wouldn't mind her ass not breathing. Call me heartless, but a nigga didn't give two fucks.

Chuckling, Big Nuke said, "Damn, it's like that, Marlon?"

I didn't have to respond to him; my facial expression said it all.

"I'm really not in the mood to beat or torture anyone tonight," Big Juke said as he took a seat next to me.

"Well, what are we going to do with him? He must take care of his kids. He's doing a damn great job taking care of *that* lil' girl," Mona whined.

Sighing heavily, Big Juke said, "Mona. Mona. Mona. Tell me something, guh."

"What's up?" she replied casually.

"Go get Markell. Then, bring yo' ass back in here an' have a seat. We are goin' to take a DNA test before I do anything to anybody," he said sternly as he glared into his cousin's shocked face.

"Janelle!" Big Nuke yelled loudly as Mona disappeared down the hallway.

"Yeah?" she called out as she walked into the room with a dark-skinned, big headed, boy lying still on her shoulder.

"Come in here wit' Marquez. You are goin' to submit to a DNA test," he told her in a demanding tone.

"A'ight," she stated as she took a seat next to Trandall, avoiding eye contact with me.

With a quizzical look plastered on my face, I paid attention to the body language of Trandall and Janelle. Seconds later, Mona strolled in with her son. Taking a seat opposite of Trandall, Mona's body language was thrown off. Right then, I knew Trandall had been skinny dipping in those bitches' pussies. Instantly, I wanted to know why in the hell he didn't clear shit up, so that my child, sister, and Sasha wouldn't be involved in this shit.

"Time to get this shit over wit'," Big Juke said as he stood up and looked at me.

"Marlon, you know I fucks wit' you the long way. That's why I'm not goin' to take their words over yours an' just do somethin' to you," he said before looking at the bitches who were sitting on the sofa looking dumb as hell.

"Then, why in the hell couldn't we talk at my apartment? Why drag the ladies into this? Why snatch my baby momma an' daughter?" I fired off as I stared at him.

"'Cause I had plans fo' each of you. Let's just say that I had a change of heart thanks to Big Nuke havin' his eyes on that lovely chocolate woman sittin' beside yo' sister."

Big Nuke and Big Juke's cellphones rang. The moment they ignored the calls, the DNA testing began. One by one, Big Nuke swabbed mouths and sealed the swabs into a clear plastic bag. Preparing for the nigga to swab my mouth, I held as much spit as I could, but I held all that damn spit in my mouth for fucking nothing. That nigga didn't even swab me.

"Wait a minute, y'all brought me out of the house to not swab my mouth? A nigga's lost. Explain," I stated, placing my eyes on the two muscular toned niggas.

"We were never at you," Big Juke quickly replied before saying, "We were at Trandall."

"What the fuck?" Myia questioned as her voice made Marlia's sleeping body jump.

"So, why abduct us for Trandall's ass?" Quinn asked in a tone I had never heard before—submissive and calm.

"'Cause I wanted him to think that we were after Marlon. I wanted him to see y'all sweat. I wanted to see if he was goin' to save y'all asses an' tell the truth," Big Juke spoke as he looked at each of us.

I couldn't lie as if shit didn't make sense to me because it didn't. I didn't know what those niggas had in mind.

"Why would Mona say that she an' Janelle had sent me a message statin' that I had gotten them pregnant?"

"Janelle or Mona, y'all can answer that question," Big Nuke announced as he took a seat next to Sasha.

At the thought of him trying to get next to Sasha caused me to growl. I didn't like that shit one bit, and I was ready to tear the nicely decorated single-family home up. Yet, I was in no position to do so since I wasn't going to win that battle.

"Because we really wanted our kids to be yours," Mona replied as she looked at the ground.

"Did y'all really send me a message?"

"Yes," they replied.

"I didn't receive a message from either of you," I told them honestly.

"Well, we sent it," Janelle responded as she looked into my eyes.

"I saw the message, and I deleted it," Quinn offered, causing me to place my eyes on her and shake my head.

"So, I could possibly be dead 'cause you decided to check my messages an' delete them? I would have been bashed fo' bein' a possible deadbeat 'cause you decided to check my motherfuckin' messages? You be doin' stupid shit that can get a motherfucka killed," I said through clenched teeth as I felt the need to wring her damn neck.

"They ain't yours, so why are you so pressed?" she shot back.

"Quinn, you are still young and dumb," Sasha laughed.

Continuing, my sassy future wife said, "It's the fucking principle that your dumbass deleted an important message that could've gotten him and those he cares about killed, fucking bird brain bitch."

"*Ooou*, an' you feisty too? I likes all dat," Big Nuke voiced in a somewhat seductive tone.

"Did you like the way I passed out when you hit me in the back of the fucking head?" she questioned aggressively.

"No, Sexy Chocolate, I didn't. I apologize fo' that."

"Yeah."

"May I take you on a date once all this shit is cleared up?" he pressed.

"Sir, what in the fuck do I look like going on a date with a nigga who kidnapped me and my family, took me out of my grandmother's home while I was cooking her Sunday dinner, in which I left the fucking stove on thanks to you, and hit me so hard in the back of the head that my shit is *still* hurting?" she sassily asked.

"Once I placed you in the back of the van, I walked back in the house and turned the stove off," he told her in a calm tone.

"Oh, how sweet of you," Sasha replied in a sarcastic tone.

"I'm really not a bad guy, Sexy Chocolate."

"Meanwhile, my feet and hands were bound. I have a stinking ass cloth dangling around my neck, which you can shove around my mouth at any moment. I don't see anything good about you so far, sir."

Chuckling, Big Nuke stood and faced Sasha. Slowly yet passionately, he took the navy-blue cloth from around her neck. Then, he bent low and unshackled her feet followed by undoing the triple-tied rope on her thin wrists.

The room had an eerie silence; however, I heard the erratic breathing coming from Sasha. She was aroused in the worst way. That was a big fucking problem for me and possibly her. The look she gave Big Nuke informed me that even though she was playing hard to get, her ass wanted to know what he was about sexually. I wouldn't tolerate her placing herself in danger because of him.

I gotta get her ass away from him, or I will have to kill that nigga myself.

Chapter 2

Sasha

Oh, my fucking goodness, get it together, Sasha, I thought as I gazed at Big Nuke like he was fucking ten-piece of hot and lemon pepper wings.

"I gotta pee pee, TT," Marlia's groggy voice said as she looked at Myia.

"Okay," Myia replied while placing her eyes on Big Nuke before asking him if he could show her the bathroom.

"I'll do it," Big Juke spoke before Big Nuke had a chance to say a word.

"Nope, I'm taking my daughter to the bathroom," Quinn spoke in an ugly tone.

"Bitch, if you don't shut the fuck up, I'm going to stomp a hole in yo' dumbass. I told you one time before it was gon' be on sight, and I meant that shit. Ain't nobody in this damn room gonna save you from me," I told her as I placed my eyes on her.

The ugly bitch smacked her lips as Big Juke and Big Nuke said, "Shit, apply that pressure then."

Rolling my eyes at them, I said, "I have to use the bathroom as well, so I'll take her instead."

I had to get away from Big Nuke. He was making me so fucking wet it was unbelievable.

"In that case, I'll take them," the fine, handsome stallion of a man stated in a voice that turned me the fuck on. Holding out his hand, I refused to place mine in his.

As I grabbed Marlia, she laid her head on my shoulder and said, "I gotta go real bad."

"Okay," I replied as I planted a kiss on her forehead.

While walking behind Big Nuke, I had the pleasure of seeing that he was semi-bowlegged. My mouth watered as I had inappropriate thoughts; the type of thoughts that I had no business thinking about from a nigga that snatched me out of my grandmother's home.

As he opened the door for Marlia and me, he said, "I'm really not a bad guy. I just have to make sure niggas know that they can't fuck over my family, an' I'm truly sorry fo' hittin' you in the back of the head. I'm goin' to make it up to you whether you like it or not."

I didn't respond as I closed the bronzed-colored bathroom door. Once Marlia used the bathroom, I did as well. After I washed our hands, I opened the door. I was shocked that Big Nuke wasn't standing at the door. He and Big Juke were standing close to the front door talking to a group of niggas. As I approached the area everyone was in, the fellas stopped talking. One of the guys glared at me with an 'oh shit' facial expression. Not knowing why he looked at me in that manner, I dropped my head and scurried to the part of the white leather sofa I was seated on before leaving the sitting area.

"Y'all really don't know who the fuck y'all got in y'all's presence, huh?" someone spat in a scared tone.

"Mane, what in the fuck are you talkin' 'bout?" Big Juke questioned.

"That's *the* Sasha Pierce," the guy stated, causing everyone to look at him followed by me.

"An' what in the fuck is that supposed to mean, Johnnie?" Big Juke growled with his eyes on my confused ass.

"*She* is our new commander now," the man replied, causing me to laugh.

"Okay, so you really have me mixed up with someone else," I said as I shook my head.

"No, ma'am, I don't. You were Charles Martin's mistress and the most treasured person in his life," he said softly while walking through Big Juke and Big Nuke.

Stopping inches away from me, he kneeled and said, "I'm assuming you didn't look in the two safety deposit boxes."

Slowly, I shook my head.

"You should. I'm only the acting commander for another week. You need to get to those boxes. Don't worry, won't a soul touch you ... even I don't know who is protecting over you."

"Can't be anyone if I was abducted out of my grandmother's home." I shot back, intrigued at what he knew concerning the safety boxes Charles left me.

"I'm the one he ordered to protect her," Big Nuke spat boldly, causing me to softly groan.

All eyes were placed on Big Nuke as my mind was silent as to what in the fuck Charles was into and why in the hell was I entangled in his shit to begin with.

"So, you knew who she was all along an' didn't say shit?" Big Juke asked curiously.

"Yep," Big Nuke replied as he placed his eyes on his cousin.

"Now, how in the fuck are you my protector when you knocked me out, dude?" I asked with a blank facial expression.

"I told you I was goin' to make that up to you, an' I meant that shit," he responded sternly.

Shaking my head, I said, "Look, I don't know anything about being a commander. Hell, I don't even know a commander of what, but I don't want my hands tied into anything illegal. That is so not me, so whatever y'all want, y'all can have the shit."

"Sexy Chocolate, I think we need to take a walk outside. We have some things we have to discuss," Big Nuke spoke as he sauntered towards me, and the guy, Johnnie, stood up.

"You have the best protector, Sasha. You really do. Peace and blessings," he announced in a genuine tone before informing Big Nuke and Big Juke that he expected them to be in touch within seven days.

The impression I received from the unknown man was that he was one of the big wigs of some type of organization that Charles was involved in.

Once the man left, Big Nuke sighed sharply before extending his hand out and said, "We need to take a walk."

"No, whatever you have to tell me, just say it here. I'm not comfortable being alone with you," I told him as my palms became sweaty and my toes fumbled in my shoes.

"Sasha, outside please," he demanded with a stern look on his face.

"No, damn it!"

"Yo' urges are showin'," he responded, causing me to gasp.

"What ... what are you talking about?" I questioned in a shocked manner.

"You know exactly what I'm talkin' 'bout, but I'd rather discuss things outside than in here. Everyone doesn't need to know what I'm 'bout to tell you."

"Yes, they do," I replied in a small tone as I gazed into his hazel-green, almond-shaped eyes.

"Since you want to be hard-headed an' shit, okay ... my task is to break that urge of yours an' put yo' mind on track, the way it should have been before yo' father decided to condition you in a way that he shouldn't have at such an early age," he voiced softly.

Without another word, I stood up and glared into that handsome man's face before saying, "Where shall we talk?"

***

"Where in the hell have you been?" my grandmother asked the moment I stepped through her door.

"Had to step out for a minute," I lied as I refused to tell her the truth.

"So, you and Myia had to cut y'all phones off and leave y'all's car here?" she continued with her hands on her hip.

"Yes, ma'am," I lied.

"You could have at least left a damn note or something. I had my mouth tuned up for my dinner, and the shit wasn't nowhere near done," my grandmother huffed.

"I'm sorry, Grandma. Something came up, and I really had to take care of it. I'll make it up to you."

"Well, it's getting late. I fixed you a plate and put it in the microwave. Don't linger in my house because I'm getting ready to have company over," she said in a tone that I found weird.

"Um … who's coming over here?"

"Now, that, my dear, is none of yo' business. I told you 'bout being in grown folks' business all the time," she spat with a smile on her face.

Knowing damn well my grandmother wasn't trying to get frisky, I erased the thought out of my head as I aimed for her bedroom. The moment I stepped foot inside, I screamed as loud as I could. I forgot what the fuck I had come into her room for at the sight of a two-piece, leopard-print, lingerie outfit and a pair of her black church pumps.

"That's what yo' ass get for going in my room, Sasha! Now, get yo' ass out of there and don't ask me no questions about my naughty outfit," she laughed.

Repeatedly shaking my head, I fled to my grandmother's drawer to retrieve the Manila folder that Charles' widowed wife gave me. As I left my grandmother's room, my mind ceased from the items on her bed.

"What is that in your hand?"

"Important papers."

"Okay, I'm sure you will discuss that with me tomorrow, correct?" she asked with a raised eyebrow.

"Yes, ma'am," I told her as I placed a kiss on her right cheek.

"You have a goodnight, sweetheart," she said as she handed me a plate stacked with food.

"You do the same, and don't be calling me in two months talking about you're pregnant. I'm not gonna want to hear it," I joked as I waltzed out of the kitchen.

"Get yo' gorgeous black ass out of my house, Sasha!"

"Love you, woman," I quickly rushed out of my mouth.

"I love you more and call me the second you make it home."

"I will."

Running back to my car as thunder sounded off and drops of rain slammed onto the Earth's ground, I made sure to protect the papers.

As I approached my running car, the driver's door opened.

When I slid into the driver's seat, Big Nuke said, "Mane, yo' grandma finna freak som', ain't she?"

With a shocked facial expression, I looked at him and said, "What in the hell were you doing outside the car anyway?"

"I was smokin' a cigarette. A nigga heard you screamin', so I ran to the porch. By the time I was gettin' ready to open the screen door, I heard yo' grandmother's response," he chuckled.

Placing the gear shift in reverse, I rolled my eyes as I shook my head before saying, "We are not going to discuss what the fuck I saw."

Laughing, his sexy ass said, "Now, you gotta tell me what you saw."

"A leopard two-piece lingerie outfit and her church pumps ... the ones with the pointy toe," I said in a low tone.

That nigga laughed from the time I put my car in drive until I exited my grandmother's street. I didn't find shit funny though. My grandmother was too old to be getting nasty with some old man. She needed to sit her ass down before she slipped another damn disk in her back. Hell, I was still wondering how she slipped two of them several months ago; she wasn't too quick to tell us how she did that.

"Sexy Chocolate?" Big Nuke called out after his chuckles simmered down.

"I told you about calling me that, sir."

"Are you gonna stop callin' me Big Nuke?"

"Nope."

"Well, I won't stop callin' you Sexy Chocolate," his smart ass replied, glaring at me.

Sighing heavily, I said, "Um, so where do things begin?"

"When you start callin' me by my name.'"

"Seriously, I'm talking about this shit that I'm involved in that I have no business being in to begin with."

"Like I said, things begin the moment you start callin' me by my government name ... Zy'Lon," he said, sexily.

Since he told me his name, I silently moaned his name several times to see how it would sound. In my head, that shit sounded amazing, erotic, and down-right spicy as shit, but there was no way in hell I was going to call him by his real name. That shit made me a little unstable in the mind.

"I'm sorry, Big Nuke. I can't call you by your real name, so it's going to take us forever to get down to business because you are being stubborn as shit. I guess there will be a lot of mad niggas in Tuscaloosa because you won't tuck your damn tail and submit to me calling you 'Big Nuke,' huh?"

"Or I can finesse it out of you without touchin' a single portion of yo' body," he growled in a tone that made me whimper.

Laughing, he continued to torture me as I gripped the steering wheel tighter while mashing on the gas pedal in dire need to get his ass out of my car.

"Say my name," he groaned in my ear.

Silence.

"Say my name, Sexy Chocolate. You know you want to," he continued.

Silence.

Snickering heartedly, Big Nuke continued to tell me to say his name all the while massaging the back of my right hand.

Nawl, there's no way he knows that. Even Charles didn't know that.

"Say my name, Sasha," he groaned before applying pressure to the back of my hand.

"Zy'Lon," I whined as my panties were soaking wet and my body was completely relaxed.

"I see now we have a lot of work to do, Sasha. This finna be one hell of a process fo' you," he said as he sat upright in the passenger's seat, still massaging the back of my hand.

"What if I said that I love being submissive in the bedroom?"

"That's cool an' all, but yo' thought process is more important. That's why I gotta get you into the right mind frame before you can become submissive in the bedroom again."

"And, how you figure that my mind frame isn't in the right place to begin with?"

"Because when I pinned yo' ass up against yo' grandmother's wall, you got extremely excited even though you showed that you were scared. Now, that's the problem. You are turned on by motherfuckas who speak in a boss-like tone. That means any type of nigga will turn you on, an' that's not acceptable. That's where you father fucked up at, but I'm going to correct all of that."

In a sarcastic manner, I asked, "How?"

"You'll see, Sasha. Trust, you *will* see," he said calmly as he continued to rub the back of my right hand.

#

Marlon

Tuesday, May 8th

"Damn, Marlon, you been super distracted. Is everything okay?" one of female my co-workers asked as she took a seat across from me.

"Yeah. Just have a lot on my mind right now," I told her in between eating one of my favorite Chinese dish House Lo Mein.

It was break time, and I sure as hell didn't want to be bothered. I wanted to sit in my car for my hour lunch break, but the rain wouldn't let up long enough for me to dash to my whip. Thus, I had to deal with chatty motherfuckers all in my face.

Once I finished my food, I had no choice but to quiet my thoughts as some new niggas took a seat two seats away from me; their conversation was interesting as hell.

"Man, who gon' take over O.G. Martin's spot?" a light-skinned, skinny nigga asked a medium-brown fat dude.

"I don't know, but there's a meeting ... Saturday at nine p.m. The location is unknown. Do you think he got one of those niggas from Tuscaloosa to take over?" the fat dude questioned.

"Who knows, but one damn thing I know ... If he chose fo' one of them niggas to take over shit ain't gon' be right. The game gon' be super fucked up. I know niggas that'll buck if any of them are in position," the skinny nigga spoke as I grabbed my phone.

As they continued to talk, I was eager to receive as much information as I could. The shit they were talking about, Sasha was in the middle of the shit. She was in the midst of her former lover's bullshit. So deep to the point that Big Juke and Big Nuke bowed down to her.

After Big Nuke and Sasha returned from outside, I tried making eye contact with her; I was still in the doghouse, so she made sure to briefly look at me, but the look she gave me was not a pleasant one. She had a wall built, and it was going to be hard for me to tear it down. No matter what I did to get her attention, she ignored me. I wanted to know what Big Nuke told her.

Unlike the rest of us, Sasha sat at a large-sized mahogany kitchen table. Apparently, she was taking in everything that was told to her. She didn't look shocked; she actually looked pleased. Two days later and I still don't know what he told her.

"Whoever the person is that's going to be the next commander is being protected and I have no idea who's doing the protecting," the fat nigga said as I pulled out my cellphone to text Sasha.

Me: *Aye, call me ASAP.*

I had fifteen minutes left before I was due back on the work floor, and I patiently waited for Sasha to respond. Thanks to her ass not responding to my calls or text, I was late returning to my working area. Finally on the ninth call, she answered on the eighth ring, she answered the phone breathlessly.

"Yeah?"

"Why in the fuck are you out of breath, Sasha?" I inquired as I hated to think that she was fucking some nigga.

"Why I'm breathless is none of your business, Marlon. What do you want?" she spat with an attitude.

"You need to watch yo' back. I don't trust those niggas. Get yo'self out of that situa--," I lowly stated before I heard Big Nuke's voice in the background.

I know she's still not in Tuscaloosa.

"Times up, Sexy Chocolate. We gotta get back to business."

"Where are you? What in the fuck is he doin' in yo' presence still? It's eleven thirty at night," I voiced in an upset manner.

"You must've forgotten what I said about you, Trandall, and Myia being dead to me. Ain't shit changed. Cease all communication, or I will be forced to use the power I have recently come into," she spat in a tone I'd never heard her speak in—ruthless.

"Sas--," I said before being cut off by the dial tone.

I dialed her number again. This time, it went straight to voicemail.

The streets is not finna turn her out. She ain't built fo' whatever Charles fuck ass got her into, and I am going to see that she is not going to fuck up her life by being a ruthless criminal.

With my phone in my hand, I called Trandall. On the second ring, he answered.

"What's up?" he asked at the same time his girlfriend, Vanessa, was going off in the background.

"Aye, we gotta link up some time tomorrow to discuss how we are going to save Sasha."

"Now, that, my dear old cousin, is *not* an option," he spat as Vanessa continued to talk harshly.

I didn't give a damn about them being in an argument; my main concern was Sasha.

"Why not?"

"Because they are settin' in motion for her to be untouchable."

With a shocked facial expression, I asked, "How do you know?"

"We'll talk tomorrow."

"Nawl, you gotta tell me now."

"Not right now. Vanessa an' I are in a heavy argument … concernin' Janelle an' Mona," he sighed heavily as Vanessa started speaking in Spanish.

"Take care of that an' hit me up tomorrow before I head into work. I won't let Sasha be involved in no one's bullshit … includin' mine."

"A'ight," he replied, not giving me time to properly end the call.

Ever since we left Tuscaloosa, Trandall had been off to himself. He didn't want to talk to Myia or me. He wasn't his normal self, and I didn't know what that was about. I didn't know if it had anything to do with the possibility of being the father of Janelle's and Mona's sons, or the fact that Big Juke may have said something to him as they quietly talked in the corner. It was a lot of shit going on underneath a nigga's nose, and I had to find out what was really going on and why—starting with Sasha.

When I returned to work, I couldn't function as I normally would. My mind was all over the place. Between Sasha and Trandall, a nigga caught a massive headache to the point that I was ready to go home and get some much needed sleep.

An hour after my break, my supervisor rushed to my side with a blank facial expression. Instantly, I began praying that I wasn't going to have to do a random drug test; I sure as hell didn't have any piss on me.

"Marlon, you need to leave work and head to Baptist South immediately ... it's concerning your daughter," he quickly voiced in a low tone.

"What's going on? Who called you?" I asked as I stepped away from the perfectly, tightly rolled pallet I was getting ready to load onto the back of a truck.

"A woman named Quinn called. She didn't tell me any details other than it concerned your daughter and the location where you need to be."

Not the one to trust a thing out of Quinn's mouth because she'd pulled this stunt a time or two before; I nodded my head as I pulled out my cell phone. I had ten missed calls from Quinn, four from Myia, and six a piece from my momma and grandma. Right then, I knew I had to clock out. As I did so, I called Quinn.

"Hello," she said in a sad tone.

Immediately, I feared the worst.

"What's wrong wit' Marlia?" I asked as I ran away from the timeclock.

"She's was badly burned by boiling water on the stove, Marlon," she cried.

"I'm on my way," I told her as I quickly ran to my car.

I didn't have time to worry about how my child had been burned by boiling water. All I could worry about was whether my child was going to survive.

As I hopped in my truck, I peeled away from the job's parking lot. Throwing the hazard lights on, I sped like a bat out of a hell. I ran two red lights before I hopped on the interstate. While driving, my cellphone rang. Looking at the screen, I saw Myia's name on the display screen. Without any hesitation, I answered.

"Talk to me Myia."

"We are at the hospital with Quinn and her folks."

"What is goin' on wit' my child?" I asked as I jumped on the Boulevard.

"Some suspect shit ... that's what's going on. Child Protective Services are here as well as the police," Myia breathed lowly into the phone as I heard my mother talking.

"Myia, explain now," I spoke, praying that nothing was done intentionally to my child.

"According to the doctors, Marlia suffered those burns hours before being brought to the hospital. There's a nigga up in this bitch with them, and the nigga ain't said a word about what happened. His body language is off, Marlon. Like really really off."

"How bad is my daughter's situation?" I asked, trying not to get pissed off.

"It's bad Marlon. They are getting ready to transport her by helicopter to UAB Children's Hospital. Marlia is wrapped from her head to her toes," she cried.

A tear slipped down my face at the thought of my child enduring so much pain. I couldn't say a single word as I zoomed to the hospital in complete silence as Myia was softly wept on the phone. I didn't have the will to end the call nor did she. The call ended the moment I zipped through the metal detectors. I saw my folks sitting across from Quinn. I didn't speak to anyone as I stood in front of my raggedy ass looking baby momma.

As I glared at her, a dark skinned nigga with a bunch of tattoos was looking me in my face with a blank facial expression. Not in the mood to address who the random nigga was, I asked what happened to Marlia. Oh, the stutters and stammering that came from Quinn's mouth was unbelievable. So unbelievable that I couldn't control my anger as I let it rip.

"I'm only goin' to ask one mo' fuckin' time ... what in the fuck happened to my damn daughter?" I shouted in Quinn's face.

"I told you what happened. She was playing around the stove, and a pot of boiling water fell on her!" Quinn screamed.

"Bitch, what was you doin' while she was in the kitchen 'round a hot ass stove anyway?" I questioned curiously as two tall security guards looked our way.

"I was in my room ... cleaning up," she replied, looking at the ground.

Quinn's mother coughed, causing me to place my eyes on her. The look I gave that winch should've made her ass fall on the ground clutching her chest. At that moment, I was ready to slap her face off.

With a disgusted look on my face, I asked the old bitch, "Where was you?"

"In my room ... sleep."

Placing my eyes on the nigga sitting beside Quinn, I spat, "Who are you? Were you there?"

"Who I am ain't none of yo' fuckin' business, partna. But um, I was there ... in yo' baby momma's bed," he spat nastily as he stood.

"So, all you motherfuckas was in the house an' na'an one of y'all was watching Marlia? Ain't na'an one of y'all had common sense to have her close by?"

I inquired as I glared into the nigga's face before I placed my eyes on Quinn and her mother.

The pathetic women didn't say shit as the nigga spat, "She ain't my daughter, so why in the fuck am I goin' to watch her?"

That stupid ass comment sent me overboard as I slammed my fists into the nigga's face, giving him a wonderful two-piece. As he stumbled backwards, falling into his seat, I drilled his face out. Screams from Quinn, my mother, and grandmother for me to stop caused the security guards to rush towards us. I didn't stop throwing punches until they held tightly onto me—damn near putting me in a chokehold. I wanted that bastard to be in one of those hospital rooms. His comment was unacceptable, and I had to let him know just how unacceptable it was.

"Marlon, please, calm down," my mother voiced sternly.

Of course, I ignored her. What she had to say wasn't important; I wanted to beat on that nigga until he was bandaged from head to toes! My ability to think clear was stripped of me the moment that nigga had some fly shit to say out of his mouth.

As the security guards held me, they tried removing me from the scene. That didn't go well until we overheard someone calling for the family of Marlia Boyd. I told the security guards that I had to be up front and center while dealing with the medical team on behalf of my child. Once they let me go, I was behind my family as they moved towards the voice that called my baby girl's name.

At the emergency room door leading to the triage, we were greeted by a thin Black girl dressed in floral scrubs, a White middle-aged woman in business attire, and two female officers—one White and the other Black. I tried my best to figure out what was about to be said beforehand so that I could prepare myself; however, the look on their faces was blank.

"Marlia is being transported to UAB Children's Hospital as we speak," the nurse spoke before looking at the White woman.

When she placed her eyes on the thin, sleepy looking woman, I knew shit wasn't going to go right. I just fucking knew it!

"As of right now, until things are ironed out, Marlia will be in the care of the state," the woman voiced professional.

Instantly, my heart began to break. Never in a trillion years would I have thought my daughter would be cared for by the state. There was no way in hell I was going to let them be over her!

"Why?" Myia asked.

"Because some things do not add up with the story that was giving by the child's guardian," the Black officer stated while placing her eyes on Quinn.

"What in the fuck do you mean the shit didn't add up? I told y'all asses what in the fuck happened. Why should my child be in the care of the state? She received burns from playing around a stove." Quinn shot back, nastily.

"A hot stove ... in which she ain't had no business playing around in the first place," my grandmother replied nastily.

"Can I have my daughter in my custody? Tell me what I need to do," I said with my eyes on the caseworker.

"At this moment, there is nothing that can be done; however, if you want to seek custody of your daughter, you will have to file the paperwork at your local courthouse," she responded as Quinn had a lot to say.

Before I knew it, I growled, "Bitch, if you don't shut the fuck up. Trust, if Marlia was in my care or my family's care, she wouldn't even be in this situation to fuckin' begin wit'."

"You better watch yo' damn tone when talkin' to my girl," the nigga spat with a smirk on his face.

The police officers told us not to start any arguments, but I ignored everything they said as I popped ole boy in the face. The tussle began again, and this time the nigga fought back. It was one hellava fight as we served blows to the face and chest before being tased by the officers.

As we were on the ground trying to get ourselves together, the nigga had the nerve to have an evil look on his face as he lowly laughed before growling, "For Lil' Boo."

Chapter 4

Sasha

Friday, May 11th

Five days with Zy'Lon Greggory was a bitch! There was nothing sexual that took place between us, only strict conversation about my urges; then, the conversation would change to us—separately. I was so damn tired of talking about my childhood that I had to sternly tell him to shut the fuck up. He refused to let me be for long periods of time before he started bugging me again.

I kept trying to tell him that there was nothing that I could do about it, which was true. Hell, I loved the demeanor of a hardcore, stern voiced, sexy ass man who piqued my interest. Even though I was heavily turned on by a man who possessed those qualities, it didn't mean that I was going to spread my legs for him. I wasn't that much of a roadkill to put myself through that type of torture. I had respect and love for my body; I wouldn't dare allow anyone into my precious temple—which only had the pleasure of having two dicks inside of it.

However, after every conversation Zy'Lon's fine self made me think about my ways, how I felt about men, how I felt about myself, and how I could potentially pick the wrong man for me based off my urges. Not liking any of the things he had to say, I kept a closed mouth as I knew that I wouldn't ever bring harm to myself. He didn't know a damn thing about me other than what Charles told him. Hell, Charles didn't know too much about me other than what he had my father do to me.

The next topic we tackled was the legal and illegal organizations that Charles ran. Things went well until we had to discuss how I was going to handle the business that required for me to manage contracted killers such as Zy'Lon and Big Juke. For Zy'Lon to tell me that I had to learn that unwanted business aspect was mind-blowing. I couldn't deal with telling people who they had to kill for political or personal gain. Immediately, I had to tell Zy'Lon a thing or two about my character.

According to Zy'Lon, Charles was contacted by wealthy people to kill those in their way. The moment I learned that Zy'Lon, Big Nuke, and Johnnie—the dude who kneeled before me in

Tuscaloosa—were contract killers and highly respected dope boys, the look on my face was priceless. I couldn't lie as if I wasn't intrigued by the power Zy'Lon possessed because I was. He noticed it and started his punishment against me—making me workout.

I didn't have to worry about the drug game because it was open to whomever Zy'Lon and Big Juke chose, which I was very sure that they were going to be at the head of the table on that. I didn't want my hands dirty in the drug game or the assassination organization. I quickly told Zy'Lon that I wasn't up for that shit. I asked him how was I going to get out of it, and his response was simple—I had to appoint someone trustworthy enough to take over. The only way for me to appoint someone was to have a sit down talk with thirty big wigs. The only problem with that was I had to know the guys well enough to even nominate them. Meaning, I had to be somewhat hands-on with the fellas and females who were on Charles' team.

Within two days, I learned a lot about my deceased lover. The type of things that I wished I had not learned. Now, I understood why his wife never signed those divorce papers—she knew what he was up too. I was shocked at the man I allowed in my space for eleven years, and truth be told, I hated him even more for bringing me into a world that I didn't want to be a part of.

Yes, Charles left me a wealthy woman. I didn't have to work another day of my life; therefore, I quit my job on Monday. I was extremely thankful that I didn't have to work for anyone. My goal of having a certain amount of money saved to have a home built from ground up was expedited thanks to my deceased Dom.

Everything that I had envisioned for myself was about to happen, all thanks to the man that I killed. He gave me severe amounts of land and a title that would forever keep money in my pockets; however, I wasn't pleased with the fact I was a commander over assassins. There was no way that my grandmother would be proud of me if she ever learned that I had people killing others for a living. How could I take lives at a drop of a hat because someone ordered for it to be done? How could I sleep comfortably at night knowing someone has a target on their back?

"Are you ready to exercise an' meditate today?" Zy'Lon asked as he stepped into the front room, wearing all-black workout attire.

"Um, no to exercising, but I will meditate with you," I replied casually as I placed my eyes on his perfect body.

Got damn, my body is sore from all this working out shit. I'll be so glad when his job is done, so he take his sexy ass back to Tuscaloosa.

"If I exercise, so do you. We can talk while we're workin' out," he growled as he threw me a new set of workout clothes.

"Look, I said I am not working out today. Last time I checked, I'm over you." I shot back with a look that made him laugh.

"Oh, so, now you're over me? I thought you didn't want any dealin's wit' the criminal life?"

Shrugging my shoulders, I replied, "Whatever, man."

"Get dressed … now," he voiced sternly and sexily.

I softly groaned. Zy'Lon placed his eyes on me and said, "You need to work on that shit, Sasha."

"For the one-thousandth time, I can't!"

"You need to, or you will be in a relationship you don't want to be in … all because of a way a motherfucka makes you feel. I keep tellin' you that," he responded softly.

"And I keep telling your hardheaded ass that I can't help that shit. So, when are you going to deal with it?" I asked in an annoyed tone.

Ring. Ring. Ring.

"You better be glad that my phone is seekin' my attention, or I would make yo' ass pay fo' that smart mouth you got," he hissed before answering his annoying device.

With a magazine to my face, I eavesdropped on the conversation Zy'Lon was having with some random ass hoe. How did I know it was a hoe? Because of his tone and what he said upon answering the phone. Whoever the chick was, she was getting on his damn nerves, but I was glad that she had his attention, even if it was going to be for a short amount of time.

"On life, you are getting on my fuckin' nerves. Every time I turn around yo' ass need somethin'. Shit, I tell you what … whatever I tried to have wit' yo' ass is over wit'. Ever since we got together, you been needy as hell. What happened to the broad that

I met? The one that loved being independent. The broad that didn't ask a soul fo' shit because she had it? I can't deal wit' this beggin' bitch you have become," he announced in a tone that had me laughing.

"What in the hell are you snickerin' at, Sexy Chocolate?" he snarled.

"Yo' ass, nigga." I laughed as I threw the magazine on my coffee table.

His focus was off me the moment he went off on the broad. Of course, they were into it about who he called "Sexy Chocolate." I had to add my two cents in by egging on the conversation.

"Get 'em, girl. Let him know you ain't gon' tolerate his tone towards you while being in the presence of another woman!" I yelled before laughing.

With an amused facial expression, that nigga hung the phone up before strolling his fine ass towards me. The moment he was in my presence, Zy'Lon threw his phone on the back of my sofa before folding me into a pretzel position.

"Let me up, Zy'Lon. You play entirely too damn much!" I screamed in a playful, high-pitched tone before I started laughing again.

"You messy as hell. I gotta get you back fo' that shit," he stated while he tickled my sides.

"Stop tickling me, Zy'Lon. I can't take it. I'ma fart if you don't stop." I laughed loudly as I tried my best to get out of the tight embrace he had me in, but I failed miserably.

"That's the oldest lie in the book. You think I'm gon' stop ticklin' yo' ass because you say you finna fart?" he questioned.

"Oh, hell nawl, you just fucked up the fun moment, stank ass lil' guh." He chuckled as he released me.

Zy'Lon's facial expression had me bent over laughing as I held my stomach. Tears streamed down my face as I replayed me farting as he smelled the aftermath of today's contents.

"I told you I had to fart. Now, look at yo' ass with a mouth fragrance of greens, ham hocks, and chitin's." I snickered.

"You sure you ain't shitted in them lil' ass draws you be wearin'?" he asked with his nose tooted.

Chuckling, I replied, "I'm sure I didn't shit, and for your information, I don't have on any draws."

Growling, I knew I struck a nerve with Zy'Lon. Hopping away from the sofa snickering, I sauntered towards the kitchen.

"Mane, we gotta go exercise, so hurry up an' get dressed," he commanded as I grabbed a water bottle from the freezer.

"Zy'Lon, I told you I am not exercising today, but I will participate in meditating because God knows I need to free my mind," I told him as I unscrewed the cap on the Dasani bottled water.

As he responded to my comment, my doorbell sounded off. Before I got the chance to see who was at my damn door, Zy'Lon's ass was acting as if my place was his. That was a big no-no in my eyes. Yes, I allowed him to stay at my apartment until our business was finished; it wasn't like I had a say so in the matter anyways. At that moment, I knew that I had to tell him that I was against his ass opening my door.

When his fine, ugly ass opened the door, Myia, Trandall, and Marlon stood at the door's threshold; the shocked facial expressions told me exactly what they thought and how they felt. I surely didn't give two fucks what ran through their minds. My demeanor towards the trio didn't change. I felt the same way I did the night I told them that they were dead to me.

Of course, Zy'Lon no manners having ass laughed causing me to shake my head.

"Now, I see why you haven't been wit' us," Marlon snarled before turning around and walking away from my apartment door.

"I'm sure you know what happened to Marlia," Myia said softly as she stared at me with pleading eyes.

"Yes. My grandmother told me, and I sent my sympathies through her and my mother," I told her blankly as Trandall shook his head before sighing heavily.

"So, why haven't you come up there?" Myia asked in a cocky manner.

"Been busy," I replied curtly.

"I don't know why we even came here. She meant what she said 'bout us being dead to her," Trandall voiced before taking a step back.

I pointed at him and said, "See, he's smart. He's understood my drift, and the severity of shit. So if y'all don't mind … I have somethings that seeks my attention."

With a brief and sarcastic huff, Myia shook her head and said, "So, I guess that commander title has gone to your head, huh?"

Instantly, I was pissed off as I rose up on her like a fucking training bra. Nose-to-nose, I said, "Oh, no, this commander shit doesn't have anything to do with how I feel about you, your brother, and Trandall. Y'all know what the fuck the business is. So, please don't get shit twisted, Myia."

Nodding her head as a lone tear slipped down her face, she slowly stepped back and said, "Marlia has been asking for her TT Sasha. Just so you know … she didn't write you off, and I know damn well that you didn't write her off because of how things turned out."

Not in the mood to deal with her or her way of making me feel guilty, I closed the door in her face. I was well aware of what took place with Marlia. I was well aware of who was in Quinn's presence when that shit took place. I was well aware of why shit happened to a baby who didn't have anything to do with Lil' Boo's death.

By me being the commander of assassins, my ear was filled with a lot of shit that I didn't want to know about—the plot against Marlon to avenge Lil' Boo's death, Trandall biting off more shit than he could chew in the dope game, and who were the top dope boys in the tri-county area, the niggas who purchased dope from Charles. The kicker was my Uncle Darrell and Marlon and Myia's uncle Henry were two of the guys who were on Charles' roster as customers. I made a mental note to check on my uncle's status as far as prison time. If he was going to receive a short amount of time, I was going to cease him from buying drugs. I was going to cripple his ass!

"Care to tell me what all that was 'bout?" Zy'Lon questioned, interrupting my thoughts as I faced the door.

"Nope. From now on, you don't answer my fuckin' door. Understood?" I growled in a tone that I never thought I would speak to him in.

"Yes, ma'am," he responded with a smile on his face.

Ignoring that smile of his, I rolled my eyes as I snarled, "Now, that we got that shit out of the way … Let's go exercise."

My entire mood changed just from the sight of those fuckers who blamed me for Lil' Boo's death. The audacity of Myia asking me why I wasn't at UAB Children's Hospital struck a nerve with me. Who in the fuck did they think I was? Surely not a bitch they could fault for some shit I didn't do. Surely not the weak bitch they may have thought I was. I was a bitch who was destined to keep to myself since those I grew up with and would beat a motherfucker to sleep over had the audacity to put some shit on me. The best thing for me was to act like none of those grown motherfuckers existed.

As Zy'Lon said, I was one unstable creature, and I couldn't agree with him more!

Chapter 5

Marlon

I had so much shit on my plate it was unbelievable. First off, I had to deal with the nigga, Deron Rogers, the nigga who was at the hospital Tuesday night. I had to fill out the paperwork in order for me to seek full-custody of Marlia followed by being at her side at the hospital. I needed to ensure that things were okay between Sasha and me. I called and texted her several times since Wednesday—no response. Since, the disorderly conduct at the hospital, a nigga had to make an appearance in court.

I was going to miss a lot of days from work. There was no way in hell I was going to be on someone's clock when Marlia was going through such a horrible time at the age of three. As usual, Quinn was on my ass about not filing for full-custody of Marlia. Of course she made threats that if I followed through with the custody issue she was going to make my life a living hell. Like the baby momma from hell that she was, Quinn didn't waste any time trying to shame me. Conversations between her and random bitches that I had slept with had me wanting to wring her neck.

I was at my breaking point, and everyone around me knew that. I guess that's why Trandall and Myia were on my ass lately too. I was a fucking ticking time bomb. The slightest look in my direction was liable to set me the fuck off. A nigga was smoking blunts left and fucking right; that's just how fucked up I was in the mental. I needed at least ten seconds without thinking about shit. Yet, when I came down off my high, my mind was on one person—Sasha. Thus, the reason I popped up at her crib.

To my surprise, that nigga Big Nuke answered her door like he was her nigga. I didn't like that shit one bit, but I knew that it wasn't wise for me to go up against him. He was the type of nigga who you had to really think about how to knock his ass off without people knowing that you did it.

"He's brainwashin' her!" I angrily yelled as I weaved in and out of traffic.

"I don't think he's doin' anythin' to her. Sasha has a mind of her own, Marlon. She made it clear that we were dead to her. The quicker y'all realize that shit, the better things will be. I'm done apologizin' to her ass. She want us out of her

*life, an' got damn it we should respect that," Trandall voiced
in nonchalant tone.*

*Trandall and I went back and forth about Sasha. The
conversation ended the moment Myia agreed with Trandall.
Extremely pissed at her for giving up on Sasha, I turned the
radio up and thought about the one female I had to have at
six years old. I needed Sasha to be in my corner as I dealt
with the court system to gain full-custody over Marlia. I
needed her to be my rock as I dealt with a child who was
severely burned to the point I barely recognized her. My
family couldn't do what Sasha could as far as keeping me
grounded. Whatever I had to do to get her to see that I made
a mistake by blaming her for Lil' Boo's death and putting my
hands on her, I had to do it.*

Ring. Ring. Ring.

Pulling my cellphone from the holster, I prayed
that Sasha's name appeared on the display screen,
but I was disappointed the moment I saw my
mother's name. That feeling went away the second
thoughts of something being wrong with Marlia
filled my mind. Eagerly, I answered the phone.

"Hello?" I said as I heard unnecessary noise coming
from her background—it was Quinn's ass.

"Son, they are going to lock this room down. Quinn
is up here showing her ass," my mother stated in an

upset timbre as I heard male voices in the background.

"What is goin' on?" I asked while approaching a red traffic light in the downtown area of Montgomery.

"Quinn doesn't like the fact that the state is looking into Marlia's incident. They have restricted her from seeing Marlia."

"I'm not understandin' why she's up there in the first place. Them damn folks already told her ass that she wasn't allowed to visit at this time. Man, I'm on my way back up there," I huffed as my driver's and passenger's windows were suddenly busted out.

Immediately, my phone dropped. I prayed that the call ended so that my mother wouldn't hear what was going on.

"What the fuck?" I yelled as Myia screamed while two masked individuals dressed in all-white held guns to our faces.

"What in the fuck is this 'bout?" Trandall asked in a blank tone.

"Just get the fuck out of the car, Trandall!" the unknown guy voiced in his face.

As I was sat angrily in the front seat with my hands in the air, I wished that I would've paid attention. I was never caught with my dick hanging out in the streets of Montgomery. Anything was liable to happen. The shit that was taking place would've never happened if my mind wasn't occupied.

With a blank facial expression, Trandall stepped out of the car with his hands in the air before the nigga motioned for him to jump into a gray truck with tinted windows. The shit had me shook because we were drawn down on in broad daylight, in an area where police and citizens of the city rode around heavily. Any other time, I would've hated for traffic to be in the area, but this time, a nigga needed the traffic to be present.

"Don't try to come behind us. If he survives, he'll be back in his funky ass city before the end of the night," the nigga standing beside me announced before hitting me in the face with the butt of his gun.

"Oh, my God! Marlon!" Myia screamed before continuing, "Please don't hurt my brother."

As he pressed the gun to my forehead, I growled as I spat blood out of the window, missing his fresh white T-shirt.

Chuckling, the nigga said, "You better be glad that I like you nigga. You better be glad that you ain't the cross in this situation."

Sitting at the red light confused, I wondered who the nigga was, and I sure as hell wanted to know what he meant by "the cross in this situation". It was apparent that he knew who the fuck I was. My mind soared as I tried to figure out a way to get Trandall out of that truck, away from those niggas.

"Who in the hell are those guys, Marlon? What in the hell are you and Trandall into?" my sister inquired in a scared tone.

Ignoring Myia, I had several questions forming in my head, but none of them could be answered until Trandall was back in my face.

"Marlon, answer me damn it!" she screamed as she hopped in the front seat with her eyes glued on me.

"Shit, Myia! Chill wit' these damn questions. I don't know any mo' than you do. When I do know, trust you will know too. It's apparent that Trandall an' I know those niggas. I'm goin' to drop you off at home. Stay away from my apartment an' Trandall's ... at least until I figure shit out. Whatever is going on ... it's some big shit 'bout to go down," I told her as I zoomed away from a city I had no business even being in.

"I know you aren't stayin' down here," she with a worried look on her face.

"I have to."

"Your daughter needs you!"

"Marlia will be fine. She can't have visitors anyway thanks to Quinn's ass. Plus, once I drop you off at yo' car … you will be headin' back up there in my place. This situation is non-negotiable, Myia," I softly spoke as I quickly looked at her.

"Don't get yourself killed for whatever you or Trandall has gotten into," she replied softly as tears slid down her face.

I hope I don't either, I thought as I gave Myia a weak smile before replying, "Never."

Chapter 6

Sasha

Saturday, May 12th

"What made you become so heavy in the streets, Zy'Lon?" I asked as I glared into his handsome face while he outstretched on my sofa.

"Life."

"Elaborate, please," I voiced as I sat Indian-style on the floor.

"My Pops was a junkie. He turned my momma into one. Some of my family members weren't too kind to me when I was growing up. They left me to die. For the ones who helped me out whenever they could, they put a nigga on to survival skills, and those survival skills led me straight to the streets. After I sold my first crack rock, I was sold on the street life. I was ten years old. When I turned fourteen, my back was against the wall as I stared at the barrel of a sawed-off shotgun Charles held tightly in his hand. He asked me one question, and I gave him a truthful answer. He helped me off the ground and put me under his wing."

With a wow expression plastered across my face, I asked, "What was the question that he asked you?"

"Why are you breakin' into my shit?"

"And, your answer was?" I probed.

"'Cause I'm hungry an' thirsty," Zy'Lon stated in a tone that informed me that he was rehashing that day.

I didn't know what to say, so I kept my mouth closed in hopes that he was going to continue telling me about his story. An eerie silence took place for several minutes as I glared at the handsome individual.

"I never wanted to be in the streets. I saw myself bein' an Aerospace Engineer. I always had an' still do have a thing fo' it but I'm stuck in this damn street life. Hell, I've become accustomed to the shit honestly. It's what I'm good at doin'," he said out of nowhere as if he was talking to himself.

"If you really want to leave that lifestyle alone, you'll find a way. Maybe, I can help you. I'm sure you have enough money stashed to go legit," I softly replied while crawling towards him.

"It's not 'bout the money, Sasha. It's mo' like I have people dependin' on me." He sharply sighed while glaring at the white ceiling.

As I bit down on my bottom lip, I had a small smile on my face. I liked the way my name sounded coming out of his mouth.

"Why are you lookin' like that, woman?" he asked with his eyes on me.

"Because you called me Sasha instead of that crazy ass pet name."

"Oh," he sounded off as we gazed into each other's eyes.

Continuing, Zy'Lon said, "Sasha..."

"Yeah?"

"I'm vulnerable right now. Will you come lay on me, so I can get my mind back on track please?" he questioned softly.

Without a moment's hesitation, I nodded my head and crawled on top of him.

The moment my head was planted on his firm yet comfortable chest, he lowly said, "Thank you."

"No problem," I lowly responded as I closed my eyes and exhaled while his hands rested on the small of my back.

We were silent and still. The beating of his heart was soothing to me as my thoughts consumed me. I was wondering how in the hell could a woman love a man so much that she would turn to drugs instead of being a mother to her child and kicking that man to the curb. I tried placing myself in Zy'Lon's shoes to see how he felt as a child, but I couldn't. Hell, I could barely deal with the things I had endured.

"I used to look up to my dad. I thought I was the luckiest girl in the world to have a man in my life who loved me and my momma," I softly spoke as I gently rubbed on his muscular arm.

I had to take a moment of silence. I wasn't sure that I was ready to confront the truth without being angry. As I felt Zy'Lon's warm, soothing hands rubbing the small of my back, I began talking.

"Family trips, family photos, family outings, but our happy family changed the moment he started acting weird or should I say the moment his eyes were glossy... always looking moist. Shit became odd and strange between him and my mother. They argued a lot, but he was still in our lives, more so mine than hers. I didn't like the odd behavior, and I told my mother, but she told me that everything would be fine. I believed her for quite some time. I was young, Zy'Lon, when he showed me how to please a man. At first, I covered my eyes, but I would get in so much trouble for doing that. I would receive whoopings, and he would nastily say that I was going to go to hell for disobeying him, so I gave in and did what he said. After the horror stories I learned about hell and the devil, I wasn't trying to go; thus, I obeyed him even though I knew it was wrong. Submission to a man, oral sex, and intercourse were the lessons my father taught me ... without ever touching me. He would quiz me. I had to demonstrate how to properly be in a submissive position and how to suck a dick by using a cucumber or a banana. By the time I turned fifteen, he tried to sell me to my ex-best friends' uncle, but my uncle and their uncle got ahold of his ass. It was too late though ... the damage was done."

Applying pressure to my back, Zy'Lon said, "I'm sorry that you had to endure that."

With tears streaming down my face, plopping onto his chest, I tried to push up, but he wouldn't let me.

"Charles told me everythin'. He made sure to tell me that he wanted what was done to you undone.

When he learned that you were pregnant, I think that's when shit really sunk in fo' him ... how they conditioned you. He really felt some kind of way for comin' to yo' dad wit' that dumbass proposition. Every day, he would call me an' ask how he could make things right."

"What did you say?"

"I didn't say anythin' 'cause I didn't know what to say to a nigga who would have a child placed in a situation like that. He had to deal wit' that the best way he knew how."

Feeling the need to clear the air about my urges, I looked at him before saying, "When it comes down to those urges, I'm not as weak minded as you may think I am, Zy'Lon. Sometimes, my gasps are just that ... gasps with a naughty thought here or there. There are plenty of men who I have been in the same elevator or room with and gasped just off a thought, but I never act. Let me clarify better ... say you see a big booty, titty bitch strolling through a store. Ass and titties bouncing, you are going to mumble or groan at the sight of her assets, right? It's highly possible that you gonna want to know how she fucks and sucks, right?"

Chuckling, he nodded his head.

"Okay, then. My gasps are no different than what you do or what a female does when she sees a nigga who's blessed between his legs wearing those damn gray sweatpants," I voiced while wiping my eyes before placing them on his handsome light-skinned face.

Laughing, he said, "Ah, so what do you do when a nigga wearin' gray sweatpants an' speak in a tone that has you aroused?"

"I motherfucking howl," I stated before laughing.

Chuckling heartedly, Zy'Lon shook his head.

"You're somethin' else. You do know that, right?"

"So, I've been told," I responded as our eyes locked into one another.

Silence overcame us as I had an urge to suck on his bottom lip. Apparently, we had the same urge because it happened. Slow passionate sucks of our lips followed by me gently sliding my hand into his messy man bun caused him to groan. Taking things a step further, I folded my legs together as if I was a frog and glided closer to his receiving mouth. My, oh my, the kisses that we bestowed upon each other were breathtaking. I hated when he broke the lovely kiss off as he lightly tapped on my behind three times.

"Hm," I moaned as I pulled my face away from his.

"That's enough fo' now," he voiced sexily as he placed his hands on the small of my back.

Nodding my head, I asked, "I took things too far?"

"Nope," he replied, shaking his head.

"Cool."

Sighing heavily, he said, "Okay, now on to the business side of things."

"Ugghh! Not again," I huffed in a child-like manner before pouting.

With a serious facial expression, he announced, "You know I gotta drill this shit into yo' head, Sasha. True, you ain't gonna be in the field long, but you have to know this shit in order to leave. I told you this already. As crazy as it is, I didn't set things up like this. Charles an' the other niggas he had contracts wit' did. I'm just followin' orders as I try to transition you out of this shit."

"I know everything I need to know. Can we at least have one day where we don't have to rehearse this shit? We have a meeting at nine o'clock tonight. Can I at least not have my nerves rattled from now until the meeting is over with?" I questioned as a pout was severe on my face.

With a pleasant smile, he said, "You better be glad that I'm startin' to love that pouty face you be holdin' strongly. No business talk 'til thirty minutes prior to the meetin'."

"Yaay!" I spoke loudly in a child-like manner.

"Get dressed an' let's go grab somethin' to eat," Zy'Lon commanded as his cellphone rang.

"All right," I replied as I lifted off his body.

"Speak to me," he piped into his phone as I bypassed my sofa.

"What the fuck do you mean, nigga?" he asked in an aggravated tone.

Not liking how he spoke into the phone, I had to eavesdrop. I needed to know was that call about me. Stopping in the hallway where he couldn't see me, I held my breath while listening.

"Put that bitch in the fuckin' dungeon an' make sure she's at the fuckin' meetin' tonight!" he yelled.

"Fuck!"

The moment he yelled, I scurried my ass to my room. I wondered who the female was that was on the wrong side of the fence with Zy'Lon and most importantly why.

"Sasha," he called out from the hallway.

"Yeah?" I answered as I quickly opened the second drawer that housed my shirts.

"There's been a change in plans. You will not be at the meetin' tonight. I will arrange for you to show yo' face Sunday. Some shit came up, an' I surely don't need you present," he angrily spat.

With a curious face, I replied, "What happened?"

"Let's just say that I have to get rid of someone before they bring down the organization that you are over," he replied before turning around and walking out of my room in a boss nigga's manner.

Running behind him, I begged, "Tell me exactly what's going on, Zy'Lon ... please?"

"The less you know, the better," he replied while shoving his feet into a black pair of low top Air Force Ones.

"Tell me," I commanded.

Sighing heavily, he spat, "No. Leave the topic alone, Sasha."

I didn't. I continued to press his ass for answers.

"The bitch I dismissed is out fo' me an' everybody I work wit'. She's an informant fo' the Feds now ... the same motherfuckas that's been after Charles fo' quite some time. The same set of government officials I had to knock off because they were gettin' too close to him. Apparently, someone told her ass some information ... only a handful of niggas was in the house the day we took y'all knew. She an' whoever opened their mouths has to die. ASAP by my motherfuckin' hands."

Continuing, he sternly demanded, "Don't dress up. Just put on a pair of shorts, a shirt, an' sneakers."

"Why would I leave the house if things are going to get messy?" I asked with a frown on my face.

"Because I ain't finna let anythin' happen to you. I don't know what I'm up against, and I can guarantee its som' shit that I absolutely will not like. Now is not the time to go back an' forth wit' me, Sasha. I'm not vulnerable anymore, an' God knows I don't want to put you to sleep again," he growled, placing his eyes on me as he pointed towards my room.

Thank you, Charles, for uprooting my somewhat calm life, I thought as I sashayed my petite ass towards my room with a sneaky smile on my face as I was extremely aroused.

"I know yo' ass got that damn smile on yo' face. Make that shit dis-a-damn-ppear, Sasha. Handle yo' urges nih! I don't have time fo' yo' ass to be moanin', groanin', an' gaspin', fuckin' up my mental an' shit!" Zy'Lon yelled.

Then, stop turning me the fuck on, bossy ass, no manners having ass, young, hood nigga, I thought as I naughtily replied, "Sorry."

"Mane, I swear you gon' make me...," he sexily stated said before he cut his sentence off and mumbled the rest of it.

"I'm gon' make you do what, Zy'Lon?" I questioned, giggling.

Rushing to my bedroom door, standing tall as he gazed at me, Zy'Lon sternly yet passionately growled, "You gon' make me do som' shit to you that you ain't gon' be able to recover from. Stop testin' me like I won't fuck you up against every got damn piece of furniture or wall in this motherfucka. Stop playin' wit' me like I won't fold yo' ass into the pretzel position an' give yo' ass a reason to gasp, moan, an' groan. Stop fuckin' tryin' my patience wit' the same damn urges I'm tryin' to teach you to control. Sasha, stop the shits 'fore I give you the royal fuck an' suck you've been destined to get from me since Charles told me 'bout you."

Chapter 7

Marlon

After I dropped Myia off at her crib, I headed to the
hood to receive information about what was really
going on, but not one nigga said a word. If there was
a time that Trandall or I needed to know something
or even if we didn't want to know some shit, the
hood spoke to us. Now, their fucking mouth was
sealed. I had no idea what Trandall was into or who
he was up against. All I knew was that my fucking
cousin was jacked out of my whip in broad daylight
into a truck that I knew was well ducked off by now.

Sticking around the hood for another thirty
minutes, I peeled away heading back to
Montgomery. I didn't know exactly where I should
go; I just drove. I hoped that I would see the truck
that Trandall got into, but I knew that was hoping
for too much. I rode around the city for forty
minutes as I let my thoughts run wild. Tired of
wasting gas as I was no closer to finding an ounce of
answers, I went to Sasha's house. Her car wasn't in
the parking lot, but I still went up to her front door

anyway. Eight unanswered knocks later, I left angry and disappointed.

Once I left Sasha's crib, I aimed for Children's Hospital. Along the way, my thoughts were on my cousin, the same cousin who's had my back since we were young. I felt like shit because I didn't protect him the way that I always had. I felt less of a man because I didn't hold my whip down. Negative thoughts seeped back into my mental causing me to fear that something happened to Trandall. My vision became blurry as my head began to hurt. Not in the mood to be emotional, I fired up a blunt and thought heavily on the things that Trandall could have possibly been into.

By the time I arrived inside of the brightly colored, chilly hospital, my thoughts of Trandall were silent as my focus had to be on Marlia. My poor baby had been through so much in these past few days. The things a burn victim has to endure—especially a child—were too much for me. I swore I was going to make that bitch Quinn, her momma, and that fuck nigga feel me the moment I had Marlia situated.

Those motherfuckers were going to feel what my baby felt and would feel for the rest of her life. My child was going to need extensive therapy, mental wise. She was going to need me to be strong for her. My folks and I were already taking the counseling sessions the hospital offered; truth be told, I needed it the most. I had to know how I was going to be able to deal with my child asking questions that I didn't know how to answer. By the grace of God, Myia, my grandmother, and my mother had a nigga's back when the counseling session became too much for me.

"What's really goin' on wit' y'all an' Sasha?" my grandmother inquired, bringing me into reality.

Myia and I didn't say a word.

"Oh, so y'all ugly asses act like y'all can't fuckin' hear, huh?" she spat nastily as she popped me on the side of my face.

Quickly, I rubbed my face and glared into my grandmother's aging, rounded face. "We messed up, an' we're tryin' to fix things, Grandma."

"Well, she came up wit' a fine ass young man, milawd, milawd," she said in an arousal tone.

Hearing that Sasha came to the hospital with that nigga Big Nuke made my pressure rise, resulting in me lowly growling.

Pulling out my cellphone, I asked, "How long was she up here wit' that nigga?"

"She stayed for a short time. She talked the nurses into letting her go in to see Marlia. She was asleep though. Sasha left her a big bear, flowers, balloons, and a *Get Well Soon* goody bag. Also, she left some money for us to get a hotel, food, and whatever else we need," my mother replied as she yawned.

Oh, so she just gon' flaunt that nigga 'round my motherfuckin' family like we ain't meant to be? I thought as I dialed her number.

The phone didn't ring; I was sent to voicemail, which prompted me to call her ass again. After being sent to voicemail again, I opened our text message thread. Angrily, I texted her black, sexy ass some lovely choice of words that I knew was going to have her calling my phone. Once I finished saying what the fuck I had to say, I slapped my phone back into the black holster.

"Marlon, Momma and I are getting ready to go to the hotel room. Call us if you need us," my mother yawned again before standing.

"Okay," I replied, sighing heavily.

Hugs, "I love you's", and kisses on the cheeks were passed out before my grandmother and mother disappeared down the hall.

Placing my eyes on my tired looking sister, I said, "Were you here when Sasha an' Big Nuke came up here?"

"I was in the cafeteria when they were up here."

"I can't let that nigga have her, Myia. I messed up by puttin' my hands on her, but that nigga Big Nuke ain't good fo' Sasha," I stated more so for me to hear than my sister.

"Marlon, I'm going to be honest with you, brother … it's over between you and Sasha. Did you see how badly you beat her? If we hadn't come in, you probably would've seriously hurt her. You might as well give up on that fairytale. You destroyed that," my sister said softly as she looked into my eyes.

Not liking what she had to say, I roughly spat, "Go to the room. You need some rest."

"Stop pushing me away because you don't like what I'm saying to you. It's the truth. The quicker you realize you lost her, the sooner the healing process can begin."

"Go to the damn room, Myia," I growled as I angrily looked at her.

Sighing heavily, she nodded her head.

My sister stood and said, "Did you find the scoop on Trandall?"

I shook my head as I closed my eyes.

"So, you know nothing about who took our cousin and why?" she asked in a low tone.

Once again, I shook my head.

"What the fuck, Marlon? What do we do?"

"I have no fuckin' idea. The main person who can tap into that type of information won't answer my fuckin' calls or texts. Sasha is the one who can pull Trandall from whatever hellhole he's in ... since she's some kind of fuckin' *commander*," I spat in a sarcastic, hateful tone.

Exhaling sharply, Myia voiced, "If Momma and Grandma ask about Trandall, you better say he's with one of his broads ... unless you're prepared for them to curse our asses out something awful."

"So, they have no idea what happened today?"

"Nope. Momma said that her phone went dead that's why the call disconnected."

"Well, thank goodness fo' her phone dyin'. I was sort of worried that she might've heard everythin' that was bein' said."

"Nope. You don't have to worry about that."

"A'ight."

"I love you, baby brother," she softly announced with a smile on her face as she made me stand up to give her a hug.

"I love you too, sis."

"Call me if you need me … I don't care if you just want to talk call me."

I nodded my head as I took a seat.

Once my sister left, I exited the waiting area in the Burn Center and headed for the nurses' station. Upon arriving, Marlia's nurse pulled me to the side.

"We're supposed to have your daughter's room on lock at all times outside of the medical team; however, we're going to go against the rules per the request from the head person in charge of this unit," she voiced softly.

Instead of my ass thanking the woman, my foolish ass asked, "Why?"

"Because someone dear to your daughter and you made damn sure that you were the only person who would be allowed in the room anytime you want."

"An', who would that be?" I asked with a raised eyebrow.

Chuckling, the heavy set, cute, nurse said, "She said that you would want to know who did this for you … her name is Sasha."

You're wrong, Myia. There is big hope fo' me an' my Sasha, I thought as I nodded my head and thanked the woman before I walked into my daughter's room.

Immediately, a smile was on my face as I looked at the stuffed unicorn tucked into Marlia's right bandaged arm. As I slowly stepped towards her, I saw a card with my name on it. I badly wanted to read the note but not before I kissed my child and read her a book. I barely finished the book before I softly cried over my baby that I probably wouldn't be able to recognize three to six months from now.

As I wiped the tears away from my eyes, I opened the letter Sasha left me.

Marlon,

I'm sorry that I wasn't there for Marlia. I let what happened between the two of us get in the way of who really is important to me and has been ever since she's been on this earth. The nigga who did this to her ... trust, he will suffer. On the way up here, I heard about what took place at the hospital. Oh, you know I gotta pay Quinn's ass a visit too. You won't have any issues being with your daughter. If you're reading this, you know I took care of that. Trandall done got himself into some shit. Some niggas took him because of what he did. I've been knew about it, but I didn't think it was that bad. I learned of him selling some fluke products to some niggas on the Westside, which placed those niggas in severe heat with some unwanted individuals. I put out an order for him to be returned safely. Keep your phone on because I gave clear instructions for him to call you. Kiss Marlia for me before you go to sleep and when you wake up in the morning.

P.S. I forgive you, Marlon, and I will always love you but I am no longer entertaining the thought of us being together, and you shouldn't either.

Be easy,

Sasha

Chapter 8

Sasha

Sunday Evening

I had a few hours of sleep since we left the house yesterday. Zy'Lon's ass had me damn near all over the 205 area code, seeking information of all sorts. I learned quite a few things that I wished I hadn't. For starters, the reason why Marlia was unattended; that sorry ass mother of hers wasn't shit in my eyes. Hell, she never was. There was no way in hell that I would leave my child unattended for some random nigga who didn't mean me or my child any good.

Deron Rogers, aka Ron, was a family member of Lil' Boo's. Ron took it upon himself to ensure that Marlon felt the same pain Lil' Boo's family felt for their deceased loved one. Little did everyone know, Marlon was fucked up in the head concerning Lil' Boo too. Of course, my status allowed me to have Ron moved to a location of my choosing, and boy was I going to have some fun with his ass—not for the sake of Marlon but on an innocent child's behalf. He was going to see how it felt to be burned and in pain for the rest of his life, and I was going to bring him the pain my-motherfucking-self.

Next, I learned in full detail what Trandall's ass was up to. He sold a large quantity of flawed heroin and cocaine to local drug dealers in the city. The issue came about when he purchased the non-tainted dope from Big Juke. That put a sour taste in Big Juke's mouth because people were coming to him talking about he was selling fluke drugs.

From what I heard, Big Juke and Zy'Lon weren't with selling unworthy drugs; their reputation of having nothing but the best was what they lived for. So, Big Juke gave the order for some niggas from Montgomery to jack Trandall's ass up. If it wasn't for me coming to his rescue, he would've been sitting in the bottom of the Alabama River. I tried to have him released within four hours, but Zy'Lon told me that Trandall had to sweat shit out for at least a week for what he did.

Not understanding why, Zy'Lon filled me in on how badly Trandall fucked up their names and money. Coming to an understanding, I told them they had to release him within four days, or their asses would suffer my wrath.

I couldn't lie as if I didn't like the little power I had, or should I say the huge power I had, but I knew I had to let that shit go because one wrong decision could cost me and those I loved their lives. On the contrary, while I had that power I was going to set some shit straight—starting with Quinn, Ron, and those who had an issue with Lil' Boo being dead. I was not going to tolerate people being mad at anyone about a death that was accidental. Yes, it was sad, but it was life.

The female who had an open mouth to an informant was the same bitch who was on her knees sucking Marlon's dick when I popped up at his house. Oh, the smile I had on my face knowing that she was no longer going to be on this earth, with her dry snitching ass!

As Zy'Lon dragged her mumbling, scary ass out of the moldy and musty dungeon from inside of a creepy-looking house, I couldn't wait to see the bitch begging for her life. I didn't like the broad from the first time I laid my eyes on her. Once he shoved her in the same ugly ass van he softly placed me in, the look on her face informed me that she knew the end for her was near. After he chopped it up with Big Juke, we were on our way out of Tuscaloosa.

I told Zy'Lon that I wanted to see Marlia. Of course, he took me; his ass didn't have a fucking choice, or I was going to use the power I had inherited to the fullest. Arriving at UAB Children's Hospital in the Burn Unit, Zy'Lon clammed up on me. His body language changed which caused me to ask him what was wrong, but he shook his head before saying nothing. I knew something was tugging at him. I pressured him to talk to me, but he wouldn't break for shit. I let things slide because we were close to Grandma Sylvia and Momma Linda.

They were in the waiting area of the Burn Center, and I found that odd. Once they told me why they weren't in the room with Marlia, I hightailed it to the nurses station with Zy'Lon behind me. Upon reaching my destination, I learned who the head bitch in charge was, so she would know that the *real* head bitch in charge was in the building. I put my professional yet stern tone on her White ass followed by calling the person who was over Marlia's case. I left a lovely voicemail on her office phone, informing her of the laws that were established to protect the parent who didn't bring any harm to their child and why they shouldn't have locked down Marlia's room. I was expecting a call from her ass first thing Monday morning.

I wasn't prepared for the sight I saw when I strolled into Marlia's room. I broke down as I held her. Zy'Lon was rubbed my back, causing my emotions to settle. Seeing that poor baby laid up, bandaged, and drugged up caused me to growl. I wanted Quinn and her fucking mother strung up right beside Ron's ass. Zy'Lon granted my wish by making one phone call.

By the time he ended the call, I kissed Marlia and told her that TT Sasha was going to fix everything and that her father would be holding her before the night was over with. Taking a seat to write him a note, I made sure to inform him of everything that I learned. I made sure to tell him that we were over, and that I would always love him because it was the truth. We had too much history for me not to love him even after he whooped me.

"Ooou, wee, there are som' dirty motherfuckas in this camp right along wit' this hoe here!" Zy'Lon sternly as he looked into the hardest faces I'd ever seen, all the while pointing at the broad who was hanging upside down.

"We're goin' to give y'all a chance to come forward before we kill yo' family ... includin' the fuckin' kids. We have a set of killers who will wipe out yo' entire bloodline!" Big Juke said before tugging on the blunt he rolled earlier.

Zy'Lon and Big Juke didn't know which of the individuals could have leaked the information to ole girl. That's where I came in. I told them to act like they knew who it was and to set a trap for them to come forward. At the mention of wiping out their entire family, I knew someone would come forward. As I predicted, motherfuckers started mumbling and looking around the heavily lit, medium-sized rim shop that Big Juke and Zy'Lon owned.

The powerful cousins looked at me, and I brought my head forward as I held a smile to my face. Big Juke turned his attention back to the antsy crowd as Zy'Lon glared at me in a way that made me blush. He had been doing that a lot since he checked my ass yesterday. I broke our intense stare by pointing at two niggas who stood with a grim look on their emotionless faces.

"Speak, motherfuckas!" the powerful cousins spoke in unison.

"Just don't hurt my family," they replied as they walked forward.

My intuition told me that something was off. I didn't know exactly what was off about the guys, but something was. It could've been their facial expressions or the posture of their bodies, but something was wrong. My mind started tripping the second I thought of them covering for someone else who didn't stand. While Big Juke and Zy'Lon talked roughly to the two niggas, I was scanning the audience in front of me. In the back row, I saw a group of niggas who had expressions that piqued my interest.

"Wrong set of niggas," I loudly voiced as I stood like the queen I was with my eyes fixed on the last row of guys.

"What you mean?" the powerful cousins questioned in unison.

"The eight niggas in the back row ... to my left ... come up here!" I ordered as Zy'Lon walked towards me.

Tuning everything out as I continued scanning the room, I saw some nervous individuals.

Wow, there's a lot of suspicious motherfuckers in this damn room. They all must go, I thought as Zy'Lon turned his back towards the crowd and placed his mouth to my ear.

"Talk to me," he whispered.

"In a minute," I told him as I continued to peep shit out.

As the guys made their way to the front, standing beside the other two niggas, I saw two other dudes whispering amongst each other. I called their asses up front as well. When they stood tall, I analyzed their facial expressions well before I looked at Zy'Lon. I pulled him closer to me so that no one could read my lips and told him what I observed. With a quizzical look, he gently pushed me backwards.

"What 'bout the others?" he asked.

"Not sure at the moment. They could have a mean poker face, or they simply don't know or haven't done shit," I told him lowly.

Continuing, I said, "Do you trust any of them? Do you have more workers who can move the dope for y'all or anything else that you need done?"

"Hell yeah. Big Juke an' I can stand to do som' promotin' if we knock these ten motherfuckas off."

Shaking my head with a stern look on my face, I replied, "Oh, no, baby, you will need to wipe out every motherfucka in here. You don't know who told who what. Therefore, you can't trust a fucking soul, Zy'Lon. My life is on the line as well."

"Wait ... what? That's twenty-two fuckin' bodies," he spoke oddly as he turned around to look at those sitting emotionless.

"You heard me," I replied as I walked away from him, taking a seat in the uncomfortable chair.

With his game face on, Zy'Lon ambled towards Big Juke. When he arrived beside his cousin, he placed his back to the niggas in front of him and spoke about what we discussed—I assumed.

With a hearty laugh, Big Juke said, "Well, I be hot damn."

Zy'Lon pulled out a burner phone and placed it to his ear as he walked out of earshot. When the call was complete, the show began; we had a nice show to put on before the main course was delivered to the rest of those in the garage. Before anyone showed up, Big Juke and Zy'Lon set up a barrel filled with acid and a deep fryer filled with canola oil. The kind of deep fryer people used to cook seafood in.

Of course, I opted to take the lead since I wanted to be hands-on when it came down to Quinn, her mother, and Ron. Oh, the torture I planned to rain down on them was fucking beautiful. Before I began my revenge against them, I zoned out as I thought of how Marlia screamed and cried from being burned. How she would feel growing up with a scarred body and no hair of her own to grow out of her scalp.

The moment my thoughts ceased, I held my head high as I enjoyed dipping the tip of Ron's head into the barrel of acid, only to pull him out when his muffled screams filled the garage. Next, I took pleasure in seeing him cry as I imagined Marlia had cried. Then, I had much delight in seeing Quinn's mother's feet dipped into the hot ass oil as her head flopped back while she yelled into the muffled clean rag that I had stuffed and secured with duct tape. I wasn't quite ready to be done with the old bitch, so I had her arms all the way to her shoulders dipped into the grease as well.

I saved the best for last—Quinn's torture. I didn't say a word as I glared at her. She was pleading with her wet, sadden eyes. Oh, the look in those ugly fuckers didn't move me at all. She had been a pain in my ass since Marlon brought the bitch into his family. I was going to let her know that I was the last bitch she was going to play with. I was going to let her know that, in the end, I was going to see her in hell.

"Quinn. Quinn. Quinn. I was going to torture you, but I changed my mind. Instead, I'm going to do things differently for you only because you deserve worse than what the other two got. I want you to care for your burned mother for the rest of your life, and I want you to give Marlon full custody of Marlia … matter of fact, I want you to your rights over to him the moment you make it home. You must suffer for what you did to that precious blessing you gave birth to. Do you understand me?" I asked, cowering over her shaking body.

She nodded her head as she mumbled, which I assumed was "yes."

I looked at Zy'Lon and Big Juke with a blank facial expression before saying, "Big Nuke, I think you know exactly what I want. Make that shit happen to the old bitch."

 Chapter 9

Zy'Lon

Got damn this commander shit looks good on Sasha, but a nigga didn't want her in this lifestyle for real, I thought as I finished what she asked of me.

The moment Sasha stepped up and let her crown shine brightly, a nigga was super logged into her intelligent, sexy, chocolate, thick ass. My want of having her increased to my *need* of having her in my life, but I had to pull her out of the darkness that quickly consumed the warm heart I was told she had. I didn't want anything dimming that beautiful soul of hers. I needed her as pure as I was told she was. She could be the one who saved me from myself. Hell, I was praying heavily for that.

"What do we do wit' this fuck nigga?" Juke asked me, pointing towards Ron.

"Hell, if I know ... ask Sasha," I told him lowly as I handed Quinn's some bandages, so she could tend to her mother as requested by Sasha.

Ding. Ding.

With my burner flip phone in my hand, I opened the message from one of the assassins who I personally trained.

Da One: *Damn, she beautiful, nigga. No wonder you cuffin' her ass real tight. LMAO.*

Me: *LMAO. Don't stare too long, my nigga.*

Knowing that he and four others were in position outside caused me to whistle and take a seat beside Sasha. Big Juke knew what my whistle meant, so he waltzed towards me. I sneakily looked around the medium-sized garage of the rim shop that Big Juke and I had been owners of for three years. It was a smaller dump when we set our eyes on it. Instantly, we knew that we could make big things happen legally and illegally as long as we improvised the old blueprint. With the best architect our money could afford, we had our vision brought to life. We would be able to kill a motherfucker without anyone knowing while having clients' rims placed on their vehicles.

It was Big Juke's idea to place windows at the right angle and height within the building; it would be easy for any of our assassinations thanks to the other buildings that surrounded ours. A unique looking button was installed into the back of the garage which controlled the windows. I loved the way those motherfuckers opened. They didn't open like traditional windows; they opened horizontally. That idea I had to tell the architect because I wasn't up for replacing windows regularly. That design enabled no shattered glass being scattered across the chosen area from one or several assault rifles' bullets.

Ding. Ding.

With my phone in my hand, I opened the message.

Da One: *Tell dat nigga to sat his ole man walkin' ass down. LOL.*

I busted out laughing as Big Juke took a seat next to me. I handed him the phone. Laughing, he sent off a text.

"I'm so sick of this lil' nigga," he chuckled as he handed me the phone.

Da One and Big Juke always joked with each other. There was never a day or time that they didn't crack on one another. It wouldn't be right if they didn't cause a playful ruckus with their mouthpiece.

"What the fuck?" voices yelled as we started seeing bodies drop like flies.

"*Oou,* look at all the peasants fall to their demise," Sasha spoke in an awed tone, causing me to look at her.

In less than fifteen seconds, the only people alive were Sasha, Big Juke, Quinn, her mother, and me. Standing, I lit a blunt as the cleanup crew strolled inside of the murder scene with body bags, trash bags, and cleaning supplies. Normally, Juke and I would leave once it was time for them to do their job, but Sasha was against that.

"Our job is done," I told her as I passed Juke the blunt.

"Your job is never done when something of this magnitude is performed. You must see that things are done properly. Like I said before, my ass is on the line as well," she voiced, not looking at me.

My fuckin' god, I can't deal wit' this woman like this. I cannot be 'round her. She's makin' a nigga wanna sex her ass up. Shit, a nigga love seein' that commander shit come up outta her, but I know it ain't best. This life isn't meant fo' her, I thought while nodding my head as my dick was rising to the occasion.

Big Juke began laughing as I wished that he hadn't.

"What's so funny?" Sasha asked him curiously.

"You got my cousin sweatin' over there." He laughed while pointing his finger at me.

Blushing while biting on her bottom lip, Sasha turned her gorgeous, dark-brown, face towards mine and softly asked, "Why?"

"I don't know what he's talkin' 'bout," I lied with a sneaky smile on my face as he handed passed me the blunt.

"A lie ain't shit fo' a yella nigga to tell … yo' urges showin' Nuke," my cousin quickly spat before chuckling.

"Urges?" Sasha inquired with an intrigued facial expression.

"He has urges just like you do, Sasha. You are a two fo' one. You been on his damn radar since we picked you up from yo' grandma spot."

With a smile on her face as she cupped her mouth and shook her head. Looking amongst the two of us, she finally said, "You lyin'?"

"Nope," his snitch ass replied with a huge grin on his light-skinned face as I handed him the remainder of the blunt.

"What triggers these urges?" she probed curiously all the while gazing into my eyes.

"You ... commandin' an' shit." He laughed.

"Since yo' ass wanna be a snitch an' shit. Tell her what trigger yo' urges my nigga." I shot back.

"Oh, I ain't afraid to let it be known that that damn Myia chick be havin' me growlin' an' shit. I need her ass up front an' center, so I can growl all up in her face," he said seriously.

Sasha laughed as I shook my head.

"I'm serious. I love a passive woman who's soft on the eyes an' will bust out cryin' in a fuckin' heartbeat. Shit!" he happily announced as his eyes roamed from different areas of the warehouse.

"You are somethin' else. You know that, Big Juke?" Sasha said with a light chuckle.

"You think I'm jokin', but I'm dead serious. When I stepped to her on yo' grandmother's porch, those damn eyes spoke volumes, an' I knew then I had to have her; that's why I didn't knock her out," he replied, throwing a shot at me.

After clearing her throat, Sasha said, "Speaking of knocking people out, you have yet to apologize for that, Zy'Lon."

Before I could open my mouth, Juke had his shit wide the fuck open.

"Nih, what a fuckin' minute ... so y'all really on the first name basis an' soundin' all seductive an' sexy an' shit when y'all callin' each other's names. What's really been goin' on at yo' crib, Sasha? Ain't no damn way y'all goin' over business. Y'all gotta be doin' som' pillow talkin' an' som' fuckin'."

"If he would stop punishing me every time I gasp, moan, groan, or look at him while biting my bottom lip, maybe, we could be doin' *a lot* of fucking," she sexily moaned in that damn commander voice.

Fuckkk, I thought as the cleanup crew announced that they were done.

***

It was ten thirty p.m., and Juke's ugly ass was working all my damn nerves. I was glad when he finally said that he was getting ready to head back to Tuscaloosa. As he moved towards the door, the doorbell chimed. With pistols in our hands as Sasha moved to the door, we were ready to blast a motherfucker away.

When she opened it, Myia stood there looking like a damsel in distress. I knew that shit fueled Juke's ass. I had an ugly facial expression because I knew my cousin wasn't going to leave Sasha and me to the alone time I had become accustomed to having with her. As I angrily shoved my gun in the back of my pants, Juke had a smile on his face as he welcomed Myia into Sasha's home as if he lived there.

Myia had her nose turned up at him causing me to snicker. She wasn't trying to hear anything my cousin had to say. Hell, I was glad because his ass would be on his merry way. Myia not entertaining him made that fool presence more annoying. That bastard stood his ground, gawking at the woman as Sasha told her to come in.

"Are you able to talk to me for a minute? It concerns Trandall," she voiced softly.

Like the boss I taught her to be, Sasha nodded her head without giving up any information. That was best since she didn't know exactly what Myia knew or wanted from her. They sauntered by us, and my eyes never left Sasha until they walked into the kitchen.

"Bruh, I ain't goin' nowhere since my damsel in distress is here," he voiced in awe as a sneaky smile was on his face.

I sighed heavily and shook my head as we walked towards the sofa. As Juke plopped his ass on, the ladies talked in a civil manner. While they conversed, I had some things that I wanted to run by Juke.

"Aye, man, do you ever think 'bout leavin' this shit behind an' goin' legit?" I asked seriously.

"Not since I was first in the game."

"Do you really want to do this shit fo'eva?"

"It's what I'm good at doin'," he responded as his phone rang.

As he silenced the call, I asked, "What if Myia gives you a chance of bein' wit' her? You won't consider leavin' the game?"

Chuckling, he shook his head and said, "Hell nawl. She'll be my lil' damsel in distress when it's time fo' me to shake a nigga's ass up ... you must be thinkin' 'bout goin' legit?"

"Yeah. I sure as hell have enough money to do whatever I want, an' so do you. Since we were young, we did everythin' togetha, an' I don't expect shit less now that we're grown, Jy'Lon."

No matter the time or place whenever I called that nigga by his government name, he knew I was serious. Thus, he looked me in my eyes and gave me his full attention before saying that we should get a handle on our tasks before thinking about going legit. He held out his hand for our sealing of a deal handshake.

I placed my hand into his as we said, "The powerful cousins."

I was on the verge of getting ready to tell Juke about promoting more niggas into the spots that were now vacant when a got damn cat fight broke out between the ladies.

"What in the fuck do you mean that he won't be released until four days from now, Sasha? You have the power to do something about it ... so fucking do it! After all, Trandall, Marlon, and I are your family, *not* those niggas," she spat angrily.

Chuckling, Sasha spoke in a voice that turned me on so bad that my fucking toes were curled in my shoes.

"Trandall shouldn't have fucked up. He decided to go against the street code, so he gets a little beating, and then he can come home. It was either that ... or death. I chose not to have death upon him so I settled for the four days. With that being said, you can actually thank the men who gave me that fucking option. Truth be told, when it concerns the fucking drug game, which is out of my fucking jurisdiction. So, go thank them and then leave my fucking apartment."

"It will be a cold day in hell before I thank them. How in the fuck can you be friendly with these niggas after they kidnapped us? I really want to know how in the fuck can you house a nigga that popped your ass in the back of your fucking head while your ass was in restraints?" Myia inquired nastily.

"Damn, shit finna get real in this motherfucka," Juke lowly stated before we hopped off the sofa, aiming for the kitchen.

We had to step in to cease what was about to go down. Sasha was liable to call me or Juke to do something to Myia's ass, and I wasn't up for that. I knew they had history together; thus, I knew Sasha would never want any harm coming her way.

"Alright, ladies ... time out. The conversation is over," I told them as Juke and I were in their presence.

While placing her low-cut, dark-brown, eyes on me, Myia snarled. I badly wanted to transform into that nigga she had met a week ago, but I couldn't because Sasha didn't order me to and the fact that I had no dog in a family fight.

"I highly suggest that yo' ass thank them for not killing Trandall as they would have done if it wasn't for me," Sasha hissed, turning me the fuck on, causing me to lowly groan.

Shit, I'm at my fuckin' breakin' point.

Sarcastically, Myia asked, "Did *you* thank them?"

"Yes, I did. Like I said before, the drug game isn't my business ... it's theirs."

"I can't fuckin' believe you ... damn sell out!" Myia yelled in Sasha's face.

Before I knew it, Sasha jacked Myia up against the wall as she spoke through clenched teeth.

"Was I a fucking sellout when I came to the hospital and threw my *lil'* ass weight around demanding that Marlon be the one to go into the room with his daughter? Was I a fucking sellout when I learned of the nigga's name that distracted Quinn from watching Marlia? Was I a fucking sellout when I ordered for that nigga to be snatched up and waiting for me when I touched down? Was I a fucking sellout when I dipped his got damn head into a barrel of acid? Was I a fucking sellout when I watched him die? Was I a fucking sellout when I had Quinn and her fucking mother snatched up and waiting for me? Was I a fucking sellout when I made sure that Quinn's mother suffered the same way as *my* Marlia did? Was I a fucking sellout when I told that bitch Quinn that she must sign her rights over to Marlon and that she would forever care for her severely burnt fucking mother? Was I a fucking sellout when I put those bullets in Charles' body and nigga-rigged the fucking wires to make the house look like an electrical issue took place?"

Oh, shit, she knocked Charles' ass off. Damn, she's commander material fo' real. No wonder it was so easy fo' her to watch a room full of niggas get murked, I thought as I quickly looked at Juke who had a shocked facial expression plastered on his face.

"No," Myia replied as tears fell down her face.

"My damsel in distress," Juke happily whispered in my ear.

As I shook my head, Sasha continued, "I wasn't a fucking sellout then, and I sure as hell ain't one now.

The only reason I won't order them to knock your ass off the map is because I fucking love you, Myia. You've been there for me so long I can't imagine going a day without seeing you ... even though I don't want you in my life like you were before."

Sasha released Myia as tears streamed down her pretty face. Myia softly sobbed while glaring at an emotionless Sasha.

Sasha stepped back with her head held high and spoke, "The way you're feeling now ... that's how low I felt when I learned that you, Marlon, and Trandall blamed me for Lil' Boo's death. That's how I felt when Marlon put his hands on me so bad that I could barely breathe. That's how I felt since I've been on this fucking earth ... a motherfucking damsel in distress. I'm done feeling like that hence me telling y'all to stay the fuck away from me. If it wasn't for me, Lil' Boo would still be here. I know that, Myia. I really do. To this fucking day, I keep thinking about how dumb I was for showing Marlon the message Charles sent me. I fault myself the moment I saw Marlon's truck smash against that pole. From that night until now, I've blame my-fucking-self for it. I needed you sons-of-bitches to tell me that it wasn't my fault. I needed you sons of bitches to not look at me as if things were my fault. I needed you sons of bitches to be there for me, but y'all weren't. But, I, Sasha motherfucking Pierce, saved the very motherfuckers who had me so got damn weak until I slit my fucking wrist in a got damn tub of fucking water. My left eye shut swollen, chest and rib cage on fire, a busted fucking lip, and a jaw that felt as if it was detached. I am no longer going to be a fucking damsel in distress … I am going to be a motherfucking damsel in destruction."

Ah, man, why do I get the feelin' that she's using this commander thing as a copin' mechanism? I thought as Sasha bypassed me.

As Myia crumbled to the ground with her hands covering her face, I knew I had to be near Sasha. There were only one or two places she would go; thus, I went to her bedroom first. As I crossed the threshold of her room, Sasha was sitting on the bed without an ounce of moisture in her eyes nor any type of emotion to show how she was feeling. I stood in front of her before kneeling. Sighing sharply, I massaged the backs of her hands. I knew that would relax her.

"Will you run me some bath water please?" she asked softly while looking at me.

"I will only do it if you put the commander hat up an' keep it locked up fo' the rest of the night, Sasha. Right now, you're very unstable," I replied as I continued massaging the backs of her hands.

"Okay," she replied as she dropped her head.

A tear dropped from her face, and a nigga had never been happier to see her showing some sort of emotion. Placing a kiss on the backs of her hands, I stood and told her that I would be back shortly. Dipping into the bathroom, I inhaled the Hawaiian scented Renuzit that sat in three different places throughout the medium-sized, blue, brown, and gray-colored bathroom. Sasha had a thing for decorating. I couldn't lie like I wasn't impressed with her taste and the African American art placed throughout her home.

Turning on the faucet in the tub, I quickly remembered that Sasha liked her water warm. After adjusting the temperature, I placed her favorite scented Caress liquid soap into the tub and swished my hands around the warm water to create bubbles.

I knew that I had to set a relaxing tone for Sasha. If I didn't, then her mind and body wouldn't be relaxed.

Leaving the tub, I pulled out a lighter. To match her signature scented bathroom, she had four large-sized candles sitting on a sturdy, dark brown, stainless steel rack. Pulling the glass tops off the candles, I placed them on the brown, ivory, and tan marbled counter. Afterwards, I placed the candles in designated spots on the outskirts of the tub before lighting the wick.

With a smile on my face, I felt pleased that I did a good job of providing Sasha with a relaxing environment. Turning off the water, I called for Sasha to come into the bathroom.

"I'm already in here," she spoke softly from behind me. If I was a scary ass nigga, I would've jumped.

Turning around, my eyes landed on a naked Sasha as she fought with a hair tie and her bushy mane. I was extremely pleased with the sight before me. Never had I seen a woman's body that was more beautiful than the chocolate woman standing in front of me without a care in the world. Never had I ever had the pleasure of being around a woman who had me yearning to be in her presence. Never had I ever had a woman who made my urges act up so badly, no matter the time or day.

"Will you join me please?" she asked after she finish fighting with her hair.

"No, I can't, but I can talk to you while you're relaxin'," I told her as I held out my hand for her to accept.

"Why won't you join me?" she questioned, placing her hand into mine.

"Because it's not the right time. You need this time to relax an' to get yo' mind right. You don't need me to distract you," I casually voiced as I helped her into the bubbly tub.

Exhaling softly and long, Sasha looked at me and said, "Tell me about you, Zy'lon ... not Big Nuke."

If any other female were to say those words, I would've went off before putting them on a list of *Do Not Call* until all pussies were unavailable, but Sasha was different and not because she was my commander.

Taking a seat beside the tub, I said, "What do you want to know 'bout Zy'Lon?"

"Everything ... I suppose," she responded while placing her back against the white tub.

"I can't tell you everythin' all at once. You gotta earn that, Sasha," I informed her with a smile on my face.

Lightly chuckling, she replied, "Okay, then, tell me something about yourself that I have earned to know."

"I'm an only child. My parents are drug addicts, which you already know. Juke an' his dad are the only ones who I feel actually gives a fuck 'bout me. Juke's mom an' my mom are sisters. I did graduate high school wit' a 4.0. I don't have any kids or a girlfriend ... actually; I never had a girlfriend, just fuck friends. My favorite color is gray, an' I'm heavily, heavily, fuckin' heavily attracted to you. Oh, an' I'm twenty-two," I told her honestly while looking into her eyes.

Sitting upright with her mouth wide open, she said, "Twenty-two? Are you fucking serious, Zy'Lon?"

Laughing, I replied, "As a damn stroke left untreated. How old did you think I was?"

"Shit, somewhere between twenty-five and twenty-nine."

"Sorry, baby, I'm a young hood ass nigga," I chuckled before licking my lips.

"So, how old is Big Juke?"

"He's three months older than me."

"Wow," she replied in an amazed tone.

With a smile on my face, I said, "So, you tellin' me that you gon' speed past the part where I said that I was heavily attracted to you?"

"Nope. Big Juke already exposed that at the rim shop … remember?" she snickered as she rubbed her sudsy plump titties.

Feeling an erection coming, I looked away as I said, "Welp, our bathroom talk is over. I'll have yo' nightwear on the bed. We'll finish talkin' when you are *fully* dressed."

"I know you aren't running away from me, Zy'Lon," she voiced seductively as she toyed with an area I wasn't ready to slide into yet.

Placing my eyes on her sexy ass, I moved my head closer to hers as I sternly yet passionately whispered, "No, baby, I'm not runnin' away from you. I'm respectin' you an' givin' us time to get to know each other. I need yo' head in a calm an' wantin' place before I snatch yo' fuckin' spirit away from you as you snatch mine away from me."

Chapter 10

Marlon

It had been one hellava week. The no visitors allowed rule, minus me, was lifted after the woman over Marlia's case received word that we stayed at the hospital around the clock. The policy being lifted was a stress reliever for all of us.

The medical team was slowly taking Marlia off medication. I hated to say it, but I didn't want her off the drugs. I wanted her sleeping peacefully and out of pain. I couldn't take her questioning me about what was wrong with her body. I couldn't take her whining and crying from them caring for her needy unhealthy skin. I thanked God every day for my mother, sister, and grandmother being present to help me with Marlia. Those women were so strong it was unbelievable. The way they handle shit was phenomenal. There was no way in hell that I would've been anything without them.

As I sat back and watched the most important women in my life care for and nurture my child, I wished that Sasha was amongst them. She would have sealed the deal on how I viewed women, and why I stressed so badly for her to be in me and Marlia's lives as my wife. She would be a wonderful mother to Marlia. I knew that shit without a doubt.

I received a call from Trandall in the middle of the night Wednesday. He informed me that he was brought home some hours ago. There wasn't much that we could talk about over the phone since I was sure that his jacking was due to some illegal shit, so I made it my business to call Myia from the hotel so she could sit with Marlia. When I finally arrived at my cousin's crib, I was horrified at the sight of him.

Trandall had never gotten his ass beat before, so I glared at him like I didn't know who he was. His eyes, lips, and right jaw were swollen. He walked with a limp, and, by the way he talked, I knew his chest was hurting as well. I made sure to act like I didn't know what he did. I wanted to see if he was going to tell me the truth.

After he told me what I already knew, I stayed at his crib long enough to see him to bed and to make sure that he was gucci. Once I was on the road back to Birmingham, I knew that it was time to let the petty drug game go. I didn't want to get jammed up in the streets for selling weed or get caught up in more of Trandall's bullshit. It was time for me to put my plans of being a husband to Sasha in motion. Even though she said that we were done, I had to have her in my life as my wife. That was the promise I made to myself at a young age.

Ring. Ring. Ring.

Looking at my phone, my heart raced as I couldn't answer the phone fast enough. Trying to hide the smile spreading across my face, I pressed the answer option as I was eager to hear Sasha's voice.

"Hello?" I spoke.

"Hey, how are you?" she asked.

"I'm good. How are you are?"

"I'm well … I was calling to check on Marlia."

"She's doing as good as she can be for a burn victim. They've started reducing the medicine. She cries an' whines whenever they touch her. She's a child in severe pain," I replied as I placed my eyes on my sleeping daughter.

"Things will get better. This I know for a fact. I'll be up there to see her sometime this weekend. I'm sure you talked to Myia, so I know you know that Quinn will sign over her rights to you without any trouble amongst other things that she and I talked about."

With a quizzical look on my face, I said, "No, Myia hasn't said anythin' to me."

"Well, talk to her. She'll bring you up to speed on things," she announced before I heard Big Nuke in the background asking her if she was ready to go.

"Yeah, I'm ready," she told him before telling me that she would call and check on Marlia later.

I was so angry that I didn't acknowledge anything else. I ended the call with an ugly facial expression. My thoughts were on what Big Nuke and Sasha had planned and what they had going on as an item. I couldn't let that nigga have what I needed in my life. Sasha was very clear that we were done, but, deep down, I knew that she still wanted to be with me. The only issue I had was trying to squeeze my way in her life without Big Nuke being so far up her ass.

That nigga was not good enough for Sasha. Big Nuke was a grimy motherfucker who didn't mind putting a bullet in anyone or setting a fire and ensuring that children were burned alive. There was no way in hell that I was going to let him corrupt Sasha, especially after all she's been through with that damn father of hers. Like I said before, Big Nuke had to get out of Sasha's life, and I had to find the right bitch that would pull him the fuck out of Sasha's presence.

The giggles from Myia, my mother, and grandmother as they strolled inside Marlia's room were the reason that my thoughts ceased. As they walked in, I had my eyes glued on Myia. Without a moment's hesitation, she knew that I wanted to speak to her privately; thus, she quickly told me to walk with her outside. Retrieving the pre-rolled blunt, I skipped out of the door with my lips pressed together so tight that a crowbar couldn't pry them motherfuckers open.

We ambled down the lonely hallways of the Burn Unit in silence. I didn't want a soul to hear our conversation. Once on the elevators, I thoroughly looked at my sister; she was glowing. I hadn't seen that look on Myia in years. I mean, a *long* ass time, not since that fuck nigga Jackson Tolley destroyed her at their wedding rehearsal.

"You datin' someone aren't you?" I asked while looking at her.

"Not so much as dating, but I am conversing with someone," she smiled softly as her phone dinged.

"Who is he?" I inquired as the elevator dinged before the doors opened.

With her face in her phone, she replied, "I'd rather not disclose that information just yet."

As we stepped out of the elevator and made a sharp left turn into the smoking area, I told her that I wanted to sit in my car so that I could take a couple of hits off my blunt. She nodded her head as she texted and smiled at that ugly ass phone of hers.

Not liking how she wouldn't tell me who the nigga was, I said, "So, you really ain't gonna tell me who the nigga is?"

"Nope," she quickly replied while delicately placing her useless phone with the fucked-up screen back into the holster.

Myia was rough on cellphones. Not a damn day went by that her phone wasn't hitting the floor or close to falling into water. After the sixth phone she fucked up within four months, I kicked her ass off my plan.

Approaching my car, I said, "Spill the beans between you an' Sasha. I know y'all talked. She told me so before y'all came back into Marlia's room."

While Myia told me detail by detail of her encounter and conversation with Sasha, I was tugged on my blunt. As my sister talked, I was pissed off and thankful for Sasha at the same time. She did us a solid by pulling some of her weight to save Trandall's ass and eliminating three people out of Marlia and my lives. For that, I owed her my loyalty. I wasn't too pleased with Myia saying how Big Nuke reacted to Sasha from the time she walked off on Myia. I most definitely didn't like hearing my sister say that the nigga had the nerve to cook for Sasha as she was in her room chilling.

Things started to circulate in my mind. My sister never said one time why she was still in Sasha's crib after they had an intense conversation. The Myia I knew would've never stayed around after an argument got heated between her and Sasha. She would've left.

"So, why did you stay after Sasha walked off on you?" I asked as I put my blunt out.

Stuttering and fumbling with her hands, she replied, "I wasn't in the best mind frame to leave, so I sat on the sofa and got myself together."

"Big Juke was there too, huh?" I inquired with a raised eyebrow as I looked at my sister.

She nodded her head without looking at me.

Chuckling, I said," That's why you're glowin'... cause of him?"

"Yes," she replied, nodding her head.

Shaking my head, I said, "Big Juke is not the right type of nigga fo' you. Cease that shit, Myia. He's mo' heavy in the streets than any of the other niggas you know. Him an' Big Nuke *are* the fuckin' streets. They ain't the type to settle down. They are built like that fo' a reason, sis."

Placing her eyes on me, Myia nodded her head before saying, "Okay."

"Okay, what?"

"I'll cease communication between the two of us," she replied before opening my car door.

I didn't say anything to her remark because I knew she was lying. My sister was lonely, and she badly wanted a companion. Myia's ultimate goal in life was to be married to a man who loved her unconditionally as she loved him with every fiber in her body. My sister wanted to build a family with a man who would give his last to her. I knew what she was after, but she wasn't going to get that from Big Juke. I knew that for a fact.

Looking back at me, Myia said, "I'm tired of being lonely, little brother. I need love outside of y'all, Marlon. I want to have a family of my own. I want to be someone's wife and mother. I'm thirty-three, and I'm tired of going to be alone. I deserve to be happy, little brother."

"An', I agree wit' you, Myia, but you are lookin' for the wrong things in Big Juke. I'm not tellin' you somethin' I don't know. Myia, if he says otherwise, the nigga's lyin'. He's twenty-two years old. He ain't finna settle down."

She nodded her head before saying, "I'm ready to go back into the hospital."

"A'ight," I responded quickly before saying, "Myia, I love you, an' I only want the best fo' you. I know you ain't gon' listen to me when it comes down to Big Juke so I'mma just say this ... tread lightly wit' yo' feelin's. If shit get too thick fo' you, then you need to leave that nigga alone. He will hurt you, an' I will have to step to the nigga an' have to deal wit' the consequences later."

"Marlon, you don't have to keep telling me the same shit over and over again. I heard you. Big Juke isn't good enough for me," she snarled as I locked my car doors.

"I'm only lookin' out fo' you, sis."

The look my sister gave me had me wishing I would've never said those damn words to her. Those were the last words I used the night she learned of how uncut and savage her fiancé was at their wedding rehearsal.

"Oh, like when you caught Jackson fuckin' some random bitch in my bed, or when you saw him coming out of a bitch's house but not before tongue kissing her? Oh, and let's not forget when he was in the bathroom getting his dick sucked by one of my bridesmaids, our fucking cousin," she nastily spat while glaring into my eyes.

Continuing, she said, "You can't possibly look out for me when you let your *buddy* disrespect me, so miss me with that shit, Marlon."

"He was never my buddy, Myia."

"Apparently, he was because you failed to be my brother, my family, when you knew what he was doing," she replied angrily.

"Look how you did Sasha an' Trandall when they told you 'bout the shit he did. You told them that they were lyin', an' that Jackson could never do anythin' to hurt you. You stopped talkin' to them fo' weeks because they told you what that nigga was doin' behind yo' back. So, why in the fuck was I goin' to tell you what I saw when you weren't goin' to believe me in the first fuckin'?"

She didn't have a comeback to my question, so I said, "Yeah, I fuckin' thought so ... you weren't goin' to believe me like you didn't believe them. You were goin' to alienate me just like you did them. All I'm goin' to say is that I told you 'bout Big Juke. The rest is up to you. I'm doin' right by you *now*. It's up to you if you wanna take my advice. If not, don't come cryin' to me. I ain't gon' wanna hear the shit 'cause I don' told yo' ass what the deal really is."

Sasha

"Oh my, these ribs are freaking delicious," I cooed as I placed the fourth bone on the red, plastic plate in front of me.

"Why, thank you beautiful one," Big Juke's dad, Vincent, happily voiced with a smile on his light-skinned, handsome face.

Zy'Lon had some business that he and Big Juke had to take care of, so they left me at Vincent's house. From the moment I stepped into the cool, manly-decorated, red-brick, single-family home, I felt welcomed. Normally, I wasn't up for being alone in the company of a man I didn't know, but I trusted that neither Zy'Lon nor Big Juke would have me in harm's way.

"I see Nuke has a thing fo' you, beautiful one," Vincent said after he chewed the spoonful of pulled pork and baked beans that he shoved into his mouth moments earlier.

"So, I've been told." I smiled.

Lately, things had turned into something unique yet weird between Zy'Lon and me. I found myself being extremely carefree around him. Like shitting while he was in the bathroom taking a shower and farting around him—that type of carefree. Those types of things I didn't even do around Charles. Hell, I was eager to cook dinner for Zy'Lon; that type of action had me on another planet. Each morning, he delivered breakfast to me while I was still in bed.

"I think you like him as well."

With a smile on my face, I didn't say anything. My body language spoke for me. One would think that I had a problem with his age, but I didn't. I quickly learned that age was only a number. No matter the age difference, if a person was feeling you heavily, you would know. Their actions would speak loud and clear, and Zy'Lon's spoke extremely loud and clear to me.

"Beautiful one, I'm not sure how much Nuke has told you 'bout himself, but I need you to know that he can be vulnerable when placed in a certain mind state or situation. If his back is up against that wall, he will clam up an' shy away. He's had a hard life wit' no one to care fo' him like he should have. I curse myself out daily fo' not being there fo' him like I should've. That's why I'm makin' it up to him now," he voiced softly with a faint smile on his long-shaped face.

"He's given me small details about himself. I haven't pressed the issue about anything because I don't want him to shut down on me. I know about his survival tactics. I know that his parents are addicts."

"Not one female has been to my home on behalf of neither of those knuckleheaded niggas. Beautiful one, keep doin' what you're doin'. He will break an' you will know exactly who Nuke really is. I'm hopin' you will get him out of the streets. It's either prison or the cemetery. Whatever Nuke does Juke does an' vice versa. 'Round the time, I was makin' my exit out of the streets, they were enterin'. I tried tellin' them that bein' that type of man wasn't worth it, but who was I to tell them that? Especially Nuke. The streets were how he survived," he voiced in a disappointed timbre.

Nodding my head in acknowledgment, I asked, "Do you know who I really am, and why I am in Zy'Lon's presence?"

"Not really. All he said was that you were a very important person to him."

Ding. Dong.

"Time to argue wit' the baby momma," he said with a light chuckle as he stood.

"Oh, wow," I mumbled as I watched his six foot three, athletic frame walk to the front door.

A pretty, fair-skinned, shorter than me woman ambled into Vincent's home with a smile on her face. She was the spitting image of Big Juke. At first, I thought he looked just like his father, but I was dead wrong as my eyes were on his mother.

"Hello," she spoke.

"Hi," I replied as I waved at her.

The moment they entered the kitchen, I was introduced to Vera, and she was introduced to me as a "special someone" for Zy'Lon. Oh, the look on her face when Vincent said that. I had a shocked facial expression that I couldn't get rid of fast enough. Seeing that Zy'Lon was her blood, she sure as hell didn't care for him much. Her attitude towards me changed drastically, and I didn't like that shit one bit. Thus, I kept my mouth closed before I said some shit to her that would shut her ass down.

Forty minutes passed before Zy'Lon and Big Juke strolled through the door. The look on my face told

Zy'Lon that I was ready to go. I didn't want to be around his aunt another minute before I spoke my entire fucking mind. Big Juke hugged and kissed his mother on the cheek; whereas, Zy'Lon barely spoke to the bitch.

"Jy'Lon," Vera called out.

"Ma'am?" Big Juke replied.

Ah, finally got his real name. How cute. Their names are similar, I thought as Zy'Lon asked me to walk outside with him.

As I stood, Vera asked, "Son, when are you planning on leaving the streets behind?"

"I'm not goin' anywhere 'til Nuke an' I say so," he responded sternly yet respectfully.

"If Nuke jumps in a river, are you?" she asked with an attitude.

"An' a nigga gonna be screamin'... *weeeee!*" that damn fool hollered, causing Zy'Lon and me to laugh as we stopped in our tracks to look at his ass.

Continuing, Big Juke said, "If Nuke start wearin' cowboy boots, I gotta wear them too. If Nuke starvin', then I'm starvin' wit' him. If Nuke start doin' dope, I'ma do it wit' him. If Nuke decides that he wants to commit a massive homicide, guess who gon' help him wit' it? Me. Like I told you before, Ma, I ain't gon' ever leave him messed up like y'all did. Y'all created two monsters when y'all failed to love an' care fo' him like y'all were supposed to. Moral of the story, I got that nigga's back through the good an' bad days. So, please stop askin' me the same questions you've been askin' fo' years now."

Big Juke's comment shut his fucking mother up, and I was one thankful bitch for how he snapped back. She had some nerve feeling some type of way about her blood. Apparently, she didn't know the first thing about being family.

Stepping onto the back porch, I smelled rain in the air. I absolutely loved the smell of rain. It brought an instant sense of relaxation and a calm spirit, something I was in need of lately with all the shit that I had learned. As I observed the gray sky, Zy'Lon intertwined our fingers as he stepped forward into the healthy, green grass. He sighed heavily several times before speaking.

"I think I have been selfish when it comes down to you, Sasha," he softly announced while looking at me.

With a questionable facial expression, I asked, "Why do you say that?"

"'Cause it's true. I'm not allowin' you to enjoy yo'self like you used to. I'm constantly in yo' space ... even though I'm in yo' home ensurin' that no one fucks wit' you. Not one time have I asked did you want to visit yo' grandmother or mom. Not once did I think to ask you did you want to do somethin' other than learn what you need to in order to leave the commander's post. Not one time did I ask you how you felt 'bout bein' in a position where you control how a person is goin' to die. Not a fuckin' single time did I ask you anythi--," he said before I cut him off by standing on my tiptoes and shoving his head towards mine, sucking on his bottom lip.

His manhood rose to the occasion, tapping on my clit causing me to groan. My actions caused our tongues to engage in a wrestling match that I had been begging for ever since last Sunday night. I had been craving for him to sensually touch, tease, and make me beg for him, but it never came. So, I had to take the lead on this one. As Zy'Lon lifted me into the air, I felt the light breeze zip through my ass before cruising to my pussy. While we continued enjoying our passionate kiss, I had my hand holding my dress in place. I was not up for my ass showing.

Taking a seat, two of his fingers found their way inside of my temple. A low, sexy moan left my mouth as it dropped from Zy'Lon's succulent lips. As he finger fucked me, I slowly rocked my pussy onto his skillful fingers. Feeling my temple become wetter, I looked into his eyes as I bit my bottom lip in a way that I knew would drive him crazy.

"Fuck, Sasha," he groaned before pulling my head to his, engaging us in a kiss that I never wanted to stop.

My back arched perfectly as my body started to shake. My breathing became erratic as I couldn't continue to kiss him. My temple became a super soaker as I dropped my head onto his shoulders, all the while fucking the shit out of his slender fingers. Not the one to hold out on a nut, I released on them as I whimpered his name in the crook of his neck.

"I need the rest of you, Zy'Lon," I cooed as I sucked on his neck and continued thrusting my pussy on his non-moving fingers.

"We ain't ready fo' that, Sasha," he replied coolly while placing a kiss on my forehead.

"I think we are, Zy'Lon."

"I said … we ain't ready fo' that, Sasha. I'm not gon' rush anythin' wit' you. I want to start slow an' build wit' you," he said sternly while glaring into my eyes as he removed his fingers from my temple.

Knowing when not to press the issue, I didn't. As I nodded my head at his comment, I damn near fainted when I watched him sexily suck my juices off his fingers.

"You taste so fuckin' good, Sexy Chocolate," he voiced with a naughty look on his face.

"I feel fucking good as well, Zy'Lon," I whined while pushing my pussy up against his harden tool.

"Aye, Sasha, yo' phone ringin'!" Big Juke yelled as he busted through the screen door with my phone in his hand.

With an astonished look on his face like a little kid, he said in a low tone, "Y'all so damn nasty."

Laughing as I got off Zy'Lon, I replied to him, "Coming from someone who watches porn at least three times a day."

"Oh, so y'all asses pillow talkin' an' shit?" He smiled.

"Would be doing more, but somebody's scared of this seasoned twat," I said, applying pressure to Zy'Lon.

"I know that nigga ain't scared of no coochie," Big Juke spat as I walked off laughing, answering the call from my grandmother.

"Hello?"

"I'm glad you're still breathing. You haven't called, came by, or even been at home. When I do call, the phone goes straight to voicemail. I know you know good and damn well I don't do no texting. Hell, where have you been? Have you heard from your mother?"

"Sorry, Grandma, I've been tied up lately. I haven't spoken with Momma. I haven't called her, and she hasn't called or texted me. Is everything okay?" I asked, feeling bad for not communicating with my grandmother like I used to.

"Everything's fine, but she's feeling down about the way things turned out for you. Maybe, you should give her a call or, better yet, go by her house and talk to her. Oh, and tomorrow, you and I should have lunch. I miss my little sweet pea."

Nodding my head as if she could see me, I said, "I will go by her house when I leave where I'm at, and I would love to have lunch with you tomorrow. Name the place and time, and I'll be present."

"Good. I'll call before I go to bed with the rest of the details. I love you, Sasha, and I don't want you to ever forget that. Okay?" she said softly as thunder rumbled at the same time I felt drops of rain on my arm.

"Okay," I told her as my other line beeped.

Quickly seeing who was calling, I told my grandmother that I would call her back as soon as I arrived home.

Clicking over to the other line, I said, "Hello?"

"Hi, Sasha. How are you?" my mother asked softly.

"I'm fine. How about you?"

"I guess I'm okay. Are you at home? We need to talk."

"No, I'm not home, but I can come to your house when I leave from where I'm at."

"Okay."

"I will call you when I'm close."

"Okay. I love you, Sasha," she replied sincerely, but I couldn't find the will to tell her what she had wanted to hear from me for years.

Thus, I said, "Okay."

Ending the call, I walked towards the porch where the guys were still talking—Zy'Lon wanted Juke to bring one of his cars down to my house tomorrow.

"You good, Sasha?" Zy'Lon inquired softly as his eyes searched my face.

"Not sure."

"What's wrong?"

"My mom wants to talk to me."

"Then, I think you should talk to her."

"I really don't want to talk about what she wants to talk about. What can she say that would change things?"

"You won't know until you sit down and talk to her, Sasha."

"I don't want to be that weak person today. Crying and shit. Reliving the past and shit. I want to be how I have been for the past week, Zy'Lon ... happy."

"You gotta get some closure, baby. Get it out of the way now, so that it won't hinder you later," he voiced while standing.

"Zy'Lon, she didn't listen to me when I told her that I didn't like being around him."

"I know, baby, I know," he soothingly as I felt emotions that I didn't want to feel creep to the surface.

Placing me in a loving embrace, he said, "I will be in the car while you talk to yo' mom. It's time to get this shit behind you. If you don't, you will never be fully happy Sasha. It's time to brin' closure to that situation an' you know its past time."

***

Pulling into my mother's driveway, I wasn't too thrilled about having a talk with her. I didn't want to be put into a mental state that would make me use my commander powers to make me feel better. Sitting in the driver's seat, I glared at the house I didn't frequent much.

"You are prolongin' things, Sasha," Zy'Lon voiced as he massaged the back of my hand.

"I don't want to go in."

"You didn't want to be a commander of assassins eitha, but I see you tryin' to step up to the plate. So, you cool wit' orderin' people to kill an' torture folks, but you aren't cool wit' havin' a ten-to-fifteen minute talk wit' yo' mom?"

Turning my head towards him, I replied, "Yep. It's much easier to be a commander than to deal with my own shit. There is no emotion tied into sending out orders."

"You think I haven't noticed when you put that commander hat on? You pull that shit out so quick when it comes down to dealin' wit' yo' issues. You are usin' that damn title as a way to do damage to people that you don't know all because of the people that's close to you who hurt you. If you would've never found out 'bout yo' new title, how would you have dealt wit' yo' issues?"

"I wouldn't have. I would've pushed them to the back of my mind like I have always done ... until things got to sticky for me."

Shaking his head, he replied, "Holdin' shit in is the reason why Juke an' I decided that we needed to monitor you since you can order us to do anythin'. Hence, the killin' of twenty or so niggas, not that I didn't mind knockin' them off 'cause you had a valid point."

"Fair enough," I replied reasonably as I opened the door.

"Go handle yo' business, baby," he stated in an encouraging tone.

Nodding my head, I hopped out of the car. It was lightly drizzling, so I took my time walking to my mother's door. The rain drops further soothed my spirit as I was about to lay my past hurts to rest. I knocked on the door several times before my mother opened it, wearing a sad facial expression as she welcomed me into her home. The moment I stepped foot inside, I saw the bastard who had me looking at porn and doing shit a child wasn't supposed to be doing. Shaking my head as I felt anger consume me, I turned on my heels.

"Sasha, wait!" my mother yelled as her hand was on my left wrist.

"I would advise you to take your hands off me," I informed her in a tone that I had become accustomed to using.

Snatching my wrist from her loose grip, I stomped away from her door—on fucking fire and fueled with hatred. My parents were behind me calling my name as the passenger's door of my car opened.

"Get back in. I'm leaving," I spat without looking at Zy'Lon.

"Sasha, I'm sorry for what I did to you. My back was up against the wall, and I had no business doing that to you. I had no business trying to sell my daughter to a drug dealer for drugs. I had no business grooming you the way I did. Baby girl, I'm sorry for not being a daddy to you."

Not wanting to hear another fucking thing he had to say, I turned around as I glared into my mother's face before I looked into his. "By noon tomorrow, you better be out of this damn state, or I will have you fucking killed like the dog that you are, and that's a got damn promise."

My mother gasped before placing her hand over her mouth. That shit pissed me off even more.

"No need in gasping, Mother," I replied sarcastically.

"You can't forgive me, and I completely understand, Sasha, but forgive your mother. When things hit the fan about what I had done to you … and how she failed to protect you from me, she beat herself up."

"Well, she should have," I told him without an ounce of emotion.

"Sasha, Momma needs us to work things out," my mother cried.

"She's the only reason you're still alive," I spat before clenching my jaws.

"Sasha, get in the passenger's seat now!" Zy'Lon ordered as he waltzed towards me. I didn't budge. I stood my ground and glared at the two people who created me with so much hatred and disappointment.

"I've always loved you, Sasha. I never wanted anything bad to happen to you. I thought that you didn't want to be around him because he didn't know how to have fun like you and I did. I never thought he had subjected you to the shit that he did. I'm sorry I never further investigated on why you said you didn't like being around him. I was not a good mother for that. I was a horrible one, and I have now accepted that. Baby girl, I need you to forgive me, please," my mother cried as I felt my commander's hat coming off at the same time my legs grew weak while tears welled in my eyes.

Zy'Lon stood behind me as I said, "I can't give you what you are seeking, Momma. I just can't."

"Then, baby girl, you will never be truly happy until you forgive me."

"Then, I guess I just won't be happy," I responded as I moved away from Zy'Lon, aiming for the passenger side of my car.

In an instant, the tears that had formed were gone as I shoved my feelings to the back of my mind.

With my eyes still on my father, I spat, "You have until noon tomorrow to be out of this state, or you will be hunted and killed like a dog."

Chapter 12

Zy'Lon

Things didn't go as I had hoped. Sasha did the complete opposite of what I had been heavily praying for since we left Tuscaloosa. She shied away from talking and expressing how she felt then and now. She put that damn hat on, and I was not pleased with that either. She had it set in her mind that she was going to have her father killed. There was no way in hell I was going to complete that mission, nor was I going to allow Juke or anyone else to complete it. Why? Two reasons—one, it was a family issue that could be handled civilly, and, two, whenever Sasha came to terms with her father's treacherous ways and finally forgave him, she might not forgive herself for ordering him to be killed.

As I drove, there wasn't a word spoken between us. The radio played at a nice decibel as the rain dropped heavily onto the windshield. My stomach growled as I passed several restaurants. I knew Sasha wasn't hungry, but I asked anyway.

"You want something to eat?"

"No, I wanna be fucked." She shot back, looking at me.

"That ain't gon' happen ... right now so get that out of yo' mind," I replied, glancing at her.

She turned the volume up on the radio and sat back in the seat with a severe attitude. I shook my head at her stubborn, hardheaded, sexy ass. I let Sasha have her little fit. She needed some time to think, so when I do come to her with what I needed to talk to her about, she would be ready to listen and fucking obey.

After I retrieved some food from Wendy's, I drove to Sasha's crib all the while munching on my Asiago sandwich. Sasha's greedy ass was fucking up her food like she didn't just have a fat ass plate at Vincent's crib. I decided to take her to his home because I wanted them to bond. I lied like Juke and I had some important street business to take care of when in all actuality that nigga and I rearranged my crib and played *Call of Duty*. I had plans of getting Sasha out of Montgomery for a while. She needed a break and a new view. Since I was her protector, after all, I needed her in the same city as me while I did my thing.

"Did you enjoy hangin' out wit' Vincent?" I asked as I pulled into a parking spot in front of her apartment.

"Yes," she replied as I turned the ignition off.

"That's what's up. You'll be seein' mo' of him. In three days, we will be in Tuscaloosa fo' two weeks ... stayin' at my crib."

"Okay, I need you to contact the big wigs and inform them that I will stay on board as commander and that I want a meeting taking place within six days," she said, looking into my eyes.

"Sasha, give someone else that commander title. You're too good for that. You didn't want it befor--," I calmly stated before she cut me off.

"I was saying what I said as an order for you to fulfill. Last time I checked, you are here to protect me and bring me up to speed on shit, not tell me what the fuck I need to do," she spat in a tone that drove me fucking insane.

Growling, I said, "Get the fuck in the house now!"

Aroused and pissed at the same time, I stepped out of the car. With my eyes on Sasha as she exited her vehicle, I tried to tell myself that once we got in that damn apartment I wasn't going to put my hands or mouth on the places she so badly wanted me to touch. Exhaling and inhaling several times, I walked towards her door.

Holding out her keys, I groaned, "Open the fuckin' door, Sasha, an' please, get out of my eyesight."

"Yo' ass gon' stop talkin' to me like I won't boss up on yo--," she nastily replied before I turned her ass around to face me, causing her to drop her drink and the Wendy's bag.

Her once angry facial expression disappeared the moment I shoved her ass up against the door all the while snaking two of my fingers inside of her hot, wet, treasure box. She gasped. I groaned. She moaned, and I lowly howled. Face-to-face, I spoke loud and clear; I talked to Sasha in a way that let her know I was no longer fucking playing with her.

"Yo' ass better not moan, scratch me, or coo my fuckin' name. You are goin' to nut on my fingers in pure fuckin' silence as I tell you how shit's really finna go down. Do I make myself fuckin' clear?" I growled through clenched teeth.

She nodded her head as her eyes fluttered at the same time her chest quickly rose then fell.

"Good," I spoke before continuing, "You the commander an' all, but I still have the fuckin' power as head assassin. People don't know who you are an' I intend to keep it that way. What I say goes. You won't make an irrational decision that will cause me to complete an irrational action. I want what's best fo' you."

"Zy'Lonnn," she moaned softly as her pretty brown eyes were moist.

Her moan did something too me. I had the need to hear her pleasure noises all night long.

"I told yo' ass that I didn't want you to say shit, an' I meant that."

The look in her eyes told me that she wanted to say something else, but the look on my face told her to shut the fuck up, so she didn't say make a sound.

"Where was I ... oh, yeah, you will not be takin' the commander's position. You will not be a part of somethin' that I'm tryin' to leave behind. You will not get caught up in the fuckin' rapture 'cause you're too damn stubborn to talk things out wit' yo' parents. Tomorrow, you will call an' apologize to yo' momma. As far as yo' daddy goes, you ain't got to say shit to him. He sincerely apologized to you tonight, so there is no need in killin' the man. I want you in my life, Sasha, an' I sure as hell don't want you as my trap queen or my commander-wife. I want you to get in the house, call yo' grandmother, then shut yo' fuckin' phone off, an' deeply think 'bout shit."

She was on the verge of nutting, but I cut that shit short when I removed my fingers.

"Why ... why did you do that?" she stammered in a child-like voice.

"'Cause I just needed to grab yo' attention since you like to throw that fuckin' commander shit 'round," I replied as I reached around her to open the door.

"Why won't you just fuck me already, Zy'Lon?" she questioned as she crossed the threshold.

"'Cause we ain't ready fo' that. How many times you gon' make a nigga say that shit?" I asked as I closed the door and locked it.

"Until you see that I *really really* want to have sex with you," she said with an attitude.

"Well, I'm sorry. You ain't gon' get this dick ret nih," I replied as I walked passed her.

"So, I can't have just a teaspoon of the dick?" she questioned seriously.

Busting out laughing as I came to a complete stop while looking at her, I said, "Mane, what?"

Snickering, she replied, "You heard me."

Sexily walking up to me, the laughter stopped. Sasha was laying it on me thick, and for the life of me, I tried refusing until I felt that she was ready to receive me. Placing herself in my arms, she looked into my eyes before softly planting her head against my chest. When she lifted her head, she walked to her room. Taking a seat on the sofa, I grabbed the remote control off the end table. Before I flipped on the T.V., I heard water running from Sasha's bathroom.

Thirty minutes later, she sauntered into the front room wearing pink and green matching sleepwear—a tank top and shorts that hugged her plump rump. As she threw her favorite throw over her body, I hopped to my feet. I was in need of a shower.

When I bypassed her, she jokingly yet seriously said, "You could've given me a small serving of the dick, ole stingy ass nigga."

If only you knew how bad I want to give you som' of this dick, I thought while laughing before replying, "Guh, go to sleep."

As I strolled towards the master bathroom, I had all types of thoughts of how I would shower soft yet vehement kisses on every inch of her chocolatey body while massaging the very places that I had just kissed. The thought of her squealing from my touch would bring me so much delight that I would go the extra mile to place hickeys in visible spots—letting motherfuckers know that she was taken. As I would happily inhale the sweet smell of her dark-brown mane, I would take pleasure in sliding my slender fingers through her tightly coiled, thick hair.

I envisioned myself loving every part of Sasha's body with my hands before I would spread her oh so smooth legs to give her hairless pussy a kiss or maybe six. With my hands and mouth, I would take my time caressing each of her fat pussy lips before slowly flicking my tongue against her shy pink bud, which would come to life within a matter of moments. A brother would do some damage—good damage though—enough to let her know that I would always take care of her body just the way she deserved.

Stripping out of my clothes, I thought of the sensual words I would express to her as I made love to her. I pondered how she would receive my need for her. I wondered how she would moan that she needed me too. My dick was hard as I thought of Sasha bouncing up and down on my manhood as her hair would wildly bounce. With my dick in my hand, I lowly howled like a bitch in heat. Never had I ever waited so long to bed a woman, but I couldn't risk rushing anything with Sasha.

While stepping inside of the bathroom, I tugged on my thick, long dick with gentle yet eager strokes as I imagined being inside of a cooing Sasha. Beating my dick with precise momentum, I turned on the shower. Stepping inside, I exhaled several times before I slightly threw my head back, closed my eyes, and went to work on my dick as if I had him inside of Sasha's hot and tight treasure box.

The more I imagined freaking her down, the faster I stroked my dick. Deep in La-La-Land, I felt a set of soft hands that brought me out of my fantasy world. Stark naked as water slammed into her hair was

Sasha bending at the knees all the while looking at me with lust in her eyes. My mind told me to tell her to leave the bathroom, but the look of need in her eyes kept my mouth sealed.

Slowly removing her eyes from me to my dick, she placed her mouth around my thick, mushroom-shaped dickhead. My eyes rolled as I bit down on my bottom lip. Quickly, I had to focus on the beauty in front of me with my dick in her mouth. My mind and heart were in sync.

While caring for my tool in such a way that no other broad had, Sasha used her warm, wet mouth to control me. When she moved her head to the right, I moved my body to the left. When she slowly moved her head to the left, I slowly moved my body to the right. Reason being, she would have full access of getting my dick further inside of her mouth.

My god. That nigga Charles made her ass a beast wit' this mouth.

The enveloping of her lips around my dick had a nigga weak, but I didn't show it. Applying more pressure to a nigga, that sexy woman began stroking my dick and balls. Everything she did done in perfect timing—the licking, blowing, and sucking. She left none of my ten-inch dick and medium-sized balls untouched. Amping things up more, Sasha's mouth became a vacuum cleaner, quickly yet gently sucking me further into her mouth and down her throat.

I'll murk a nigga 'bout yo' ass, Sasha. Ain't no way I'mma let you just up an' leave me.

"Fuck!" I growled loudly as I was stuck in place while glaring at the beautiful creature.

Slowly dragging her mouth from the base of my dick, she cockily asked, "You like that, Zy'Lon?"

Hell yes. This the type of shit that'll have me actin' stupid.

She didn't give me a chance to respond because she began humming on my dick, sending vibrations and tingling sensations throughout my entire body. A nigga couldn't even nod his head for the ultimate satisfaction I was receiving. I wanted to groan and tell her how good it felt, but I felt like I would be a punk nigga for speaking out during sex other than occasionally saying "fuck", "shit", or "got damn". All I could do was look at her with an awed facial expression.

Within a matter of moments, my core shook as Sasha *yum'med* and *mmm'ed* as my little boys and girls slid down her throat while she massaged my balls.

What the fuck! Game over. There is no way in hell I can refuse her sex now.

Once she finished, Sasha stood with a smile on her face before saying, "I didn't think it was fair for you to make me cum twice, and you had to make yourself cum. Now, we can go to sleep."

Taken aback by her statement, I said, "I'm ready to give you a *teaspoon* of dick, now."

As she stepped out of the shower, shaking her head, Sasha softly and seductively laughed before saying, "Nope, we ain't ready yet. Remember?"

Chuckling, I let her ass leave the bathroom, but I had to give it to her. She turned the tables in her favor, but I knew just how to get her slim-thick ass. Several minutes passed and I was still thinking about sexing her; thus, I finished cleaning my body so that I could make that happen. After drying off, I secured the towel around my waist. While retrieving my toothbrush and toothpaste, I wiped off the steam-filled mirror. Ensuring I took care of my mouth properly, I did so as I listened to slow jams playing lowly from Sasha's room.

Oh, she tryin' to set the mood, huh? I thought while I spit out the excess toothpaste, only to resume cleaning my mouth.

Once I finished, I cleaned the bathtub and dried the floor. Pleased at the cleanup of the bathroom, I sauntered into the master bedroom. The sight before my eyes had a smile on my face. Sasha was lying underneath the covers, glaring at me. She was naked just like she had been sleeping since I arrived. She absolutely hated having clothes on, which I tried to break her out of. After the second day, I just said fuck it; after all, she was in her crib.

"I'm sleepy, Zy'Lon. Will you hold me until I fall asleep?" she asked softly as I stared at her.

"Do you always gotta ask me that question every day an' night, woman?"

"Yep."

"Well, I wish you would stop. I know you like to be held when you're sleepy," I joked in a playful manner as I removed the towel from around my waist.

With her eyes on me, Sasha moved towards the other side of the bed. As I climbed in, she sat upright, looking at me with calm eyes. While lying onto the firm, cold pillows, I pulled Sasha towards me. Instead of her lying in the crook of my arm, she climbed on top of me. Her wild mane tickled my chin as I felt her heavily sighing, something that she did regularly when she laid on top of me.

I remained quiet as I knew my heartbeat was putting her to sleep. Going the extra mile, I massaged her back with the right amount of pressure. Before I knew it, Sasha was softly snoring.

With a content facial expression plastered across my handsome face, I said, "Goodnight, Sasha."

I was still riled from her bathroom antics, so it took me a while to fall asleep. The soft melodies of old school jams played as some of the songs brought back childhood memories—some good, some bad. The bad outweighed the good, causing me to become vulnerable. As I rehashed the memories, I thought of ways that my life could have went differently. Seeing that there wasn't a way, I stopped worrying about my past because it was what it was—a past that had made me strong and weak at the same time. One of my favorite songs by Sade played, bringing calmness to my soul—her soft voice and the tune of her songs always did.

I didn't know how long I was asleep, but I was awakened by Sasha slowly rocking on my dick as she whispered, "Wake up for me, Zy'Lon. I'm tired of you holding out on me."

A nigga's dick was dripping wet with her sweet, sticky juices. I was discombobulated than a motherfucker, and the top of my head was hurting. Trying to understand why my head was hurting, I had a crazy look on my face as my body rocked back and forth.

This damn woman don' fucked the shit out of me while I was sleepin'. My fuckin' head hittin' the headboard an' shit. Oh, hell nawl.

"'Bout time you wake up," she sexily whined while pussy popping on the head of my dick.

"Woman, did you bang my head up against the headboard?" I asked, thrusting my dick into the corner of her pussy that called for me to be there.

"Yep," she giggled sexily before biting on my bottom lip.

"You took pleasure in that, huh?" I questioned as my right hand grabbed that juicy ass of hers while my left hand was full of her tightly coiled hair.

As I slammed my dick further into Sasha's treasure box, she loudly cooed, "Yesss."

Not knowing how long she had been fucking a nigga in his sleep, I roughly placed her on her back. Removing my manhood from her hole, she whined for me to put him back in.

"Nawl, I can't do that right now," I said, sucking on her neck.

Everything that I imagined I would do to Sasha, I did. Everything I prepared to say to her while I was pleasing her body, I did. Her reaction to my words and actions were priceless. She had me gone as I knew I had her gone. We belonged to each other. Her soul was mine as mine was hers—just the way I intended it to be.

Chapter 13

Sasha

Wednesday, May 23rd

When I woke up this morning, my spirit was feeling refreshed. Yesterday, I sincerely apologized to my mother; however, I hadn't forgiven her. It was going to take time for me to forgive her.

Lunch with my grandmother was great. She had chosen to eat at The Catfish House in Millbrook. We talked about everything that I had endured as a child and possibly as an adult. I didn't deny anything that she said; she was correct. By the end of our conversation, I had decided that it was in my best interest to try to forgive my parents. My grandmother had suggested that I sit down and talk with them. Without a doubt in my mind, that shit wasn't going to go well; thus, I told her that I wasn't up for either of them being in my face at the moment.

"Listen, girl, you want me, but he needs you," Zy'Lon sang along with R. Kelly's song "Down Low."

That nigga had a voice on him. Instantly, I became a fucking groupie. I was all over him as he sang while dancing with me. I was like a school girl dancing with her crush, smiling and blushing. Afterwards, we joyfully cleaned and rearranged the furniture. Before he entered my life, I hated the deep cleaning that I did once a month. I hated moving furniture. That shit was time consuming and had me tired as fuck, but he turned it into a fun activity with his goofy ass ways. The moment he turned on the radio, things went smoothly. We rapped along to trap songs, danced when slow jams played, and I twerked on him when an ass shaking, titty bouncing song came on.

"I see someone is enjoyin' deep cleanin' day, huh?" Zy'Lon said as "Nuthin' But A G Thang" by Dr. Dre and Snoop Dogg ended.

"Some like that," I replied with a smile on my face as I heard the beat of one of my cut-up jams.

My eyes were wide as my body went into super crunk mode the moment I heard Webbie's voice blasting through my speakers saying, "I'm that nigga, ya' fuckin' right."

Immediately, I rapped along to Webbie's "You Bitch".

"Okay nih, Sexy Chocolate!" Zy'Lon loudly said, bobbing his head and jigging to the song all the while sexily strolling towards me.

"Ayee!" I bobbed my head while bouncing my body to the beat that blasted from the speakers of my radio.

Aggressively throwing the large-sized throw pills on the sofa that we rearranged closer to the balcony doors, I playfully mean mugged Zy'Lon as he laughed and shook his head at me.

"You bitch, you bitch, you bitch!" we yelled in unison as we pointed at the ceiling.

In need of feeling him closer to me, I scooted my ass up to his six foot two frame. His dick print was looking mighty delicious as his tool moved from him jigging to the song. Licking my lips, I sexily rapped the words. I gave his ass so much thuggish yet sexy sex appeal that he pulled me close, dropping a hungry kiss on my lips that had me wanting more of him. Ever since Monday night, I couldn't keep my hands off him. He tried to not to give me two teaspoons of his dick, but in the end I would win.

Pulling away from me, Zy'Lon shook his head and said, "You ain't gettin' none nih. You always tryin' to molest me an' shit. I said, 'no'."

Laughing, I replied, "I ain't even trying to do nothing."

"A lie ain't shit fo' a sexy woman to tell. I know yo' moves nih. You get to runnin' yo' damn hands across the back of my head an' hold that motherfucka tight. I know you want a teaspoon of this dick. Ya ass ain't gettin' none *tah-damn-day*," he chuckled as he backed away with his hands in the air.

"Whatever, Zy'Lon. You know just like I know whenever I want it all I gotta do is put this mouth on you," I said cockily.

"See," he said, pointing at me, "You ain't fair. You know damn well that wet, warm, vacuum cleaner on you don't play the radio wit' me. That's why I started sleepin' on the damn sofa."

"Yo' ass ain't safe on the sofa either; hence, this morning," I snickered as we resumed last of the cleaning in the front room.

"You gon' make shit hard fo' a nigga, huh?" he asked as his cellphone rang.

"I disagree."

Chuckling, he said, "You would, wouldn't you?"

Ignoring his phone, Zy'Lon changed the subject as we removed the books off my cherry oak bookshelf.

"So, 'bout this commander thing ... have you selected a person to take over yet?"

Sighing heavily, I was tired of him bringing it up. I knew that he didn't want me in that life, but I sort of liked it. I wasn't going to tell him that I wanted to keep the title because he had a way of making me rethink things the moment he shove me up against the wall, the sofa, or the kitchen table and made me shout and fight for him to make me cum all over his fingers. In order for me to cum, I would have to tell him that I didn't want the title. If I kept up the act of wanting it, he would bring me close to an orgasm before removing his fingers, and I would be mad as hell. Eventually, I would give in and tell him that I wouldn't keep the title all for that damn nut.

"Um, I think so," I replied, not looking at him.

"Yo' ass ain't thought 'bout shit, have you?" he asked before laughing.

Shaking my head, I said, "Not really."

"Yo' time runnin' out, Sasha. Like I told you before, I don't want you participatin' in this lifestyle. You was never meant to be in it in the first place. This shit can turn you cold as hell, an' you don't deserve to be turned cold," he spoke in a loving tone.

Just like he wanted me to leave the lifestyle alone, I wanted the same for him. Zy'Lon was so intelligent that he didn't need to be a killer or a drug supplier. He had the potential to make a difference in the African American community; he had a voice that people would listen to and follow behind him through hell or high water. He was the man illegally and legally. He was such a powerful being. I just had to show him how powerful he really was. He could make a difference if anyone else couldn't.

"I will make you a deal," I said as I softly placed my hardback books on the clean carpet before continuing, "You start transitioning out of that lifestyle, and I will give you a person to put on the commander's throne."

"Like I told you before, hardheaded woman, I can't transition out right now. I probably won't be able to leave this life fo' at least another year or two. My hands are tied into som' shit that has to be dealt wit' first. My main priority is gettin' you out of that hellish position."

Without attitude, I said, "Zy'Lon, I'm not leaving this position until you make the first initial step of going after what you've always wanted ... a better life for yourself and others. You could employ thousands of people and have them living comfortably ... the legit way."

"I said what I said, Sasha," he sternly replied as he looked at me with a raised eyebrow.

Rolling my eyes at his ass, silence overcame us as "Bedroom Boom" by Ying Yang Twins featuring Avant played. Normally, when a song of that nature played, I would tease Zy'Lon; however, this go-round, we weren't seeing eye-to-eye. He was being stubborn, and I was pouty and quiet.

After we finished our tasks, I strolled towards the kitchen. It was my turn to cook dinner, so I had to see what I was in the mood to fix. As I opened the freezer, I sighed heavily as I skimmed through the different meats. Not in the mood for chicken, pork chops, ribs, or a roast, I selected two packs of ground beef. Placing them in a deep-dish pan filled with cold water, I opened the refrigerator to see if I had any onions and bell peppers. Seeing that I did, I knew that my meal of homemade meatloaf was a go. For

dessert, I decided on homemade banana pudding—
Zy'Lon's favorite. After realizing that I didn't have
any bananas or vanilla wafers, I called out to Zy'Lon.

He didn't answer, so I called his name again. His
ass still didn't answer me. Skipping out of the
kitchen, I saw that he wasn't in the front room; thus,
I ambled towards my room. The closer I got to my
newly rearranged room I heard the shower going as
Zy'Lon talked. By the aggressive way he spoke, I
knew he was on the phone with Big Juke.

"Well, we gotta do som' fast. She ain't gon' leave the
commander's position 'til I make som' type of effort
to leave the lifestyle. I ain't tryin' to lose her, nigga.
With that being said, you need to be headin' ya' ugly
ass down here. We can see how we can set som' shit
into motion."

Apparently, Big Juke started joking because Zy'Lon
replied, "Fuck you, nigga. At least, I can say I'm pussy
whipped an' lovin' it, can you? Fuck nawl. 'Cause
Myia ain't finna give you none of that twat that yo'
ass been beggin' fo'. Nih, fuck nigga, get the fuck off
my line an' get my truck down here."

My head was on swole mode after hearing Zy'Lon
say that he wasn't trying to lose me and that he was

pussy whipped; that let me know that the little feelings we had accrued were real and not some spur of the moment type of shit. As they joked and laughed, it brought back memories of how Trandall, Marlon, Myia, and I used to be on three-way whenever our summer vacations were over. Those memories caused me to wish that things didn't turn out the way that they did between us.

Sad emotions tried to sneak up on me, but I stopped the thoughts of how badly I missed them from putting a damper on my day. Rapidly coming out of my clothes as Zy'Lon and Big Juke chatted on the phone, I was in need of having my mood changed. Sauntering my ass into the bathroom, I damn near gagged at the scent that hit my nose.

"'Ole, shitty booty ass nigga," I laughed as I placed a finger underneath my nostrils while looking at his fine self on the toilet.

"Shut yo' ass up an' get in the tub, guh." He laughed.

I didn't know what Big Juke told his ass that had him laughing so hard before he said, "You ain't shit fo' that comment, nigga. Brang me my shit fo' it be som' problems."

As I sexily walked towards the tub, he ended the call. With my eyes on Zy'Lon, I gave him the 'fuck me' facial expression.

"Nope!" he voiced loudly.

Laughing, I said, "You always say 'nope' but I still end up getting it anyways."

I seductively entered the tub all the while watching him. I didn't last three damn seconds before I quickly jumped out as if a thousand snakes were in the fucking shower and yelled, "That fucking water is too got damn hot, Zy'Lon! What the fuck!"

"I didn't think you were goin' to join me," he replied while laughing.

As I rolled my eyes, he asked, "Will you get out, so I can wipe my ass in peace please?"

"Nope. You don't get out when I have to wipe my ass." I shot back with a smirk on my face as I adjusted the temperature of the water.

"Mane, Sasha, I'm serious. Please, get out the bathroom."

"I said ... no," I giggled as I looked at him.

"Mane, you play too fuckin' much," he replied while shaking his head. "Look, I'll give you a teaspoon of dick on demand ... if yo' ass leave the bathroom, so I can handle my business."

With a raised eyebrow as I stuck my hand underneath the showerhead, I shook my head and said, "I can get that dick whenever I want. All I gotta do is make yo' toes curl with this mouth of mine, or I can speak in that tone that have your dick and patience on beast mode."

"Maanne," he said before I slipped into the shower.

Chuckling, I replied, "Yep, I win ... again."

I knew how men were when it came down to wiping their asses after they'd shitted, so I respected his privacy. As I grabbed my black loofah, the toilet flushed. Like always after shitting, Zy'Lon began whistling while turning on the water in the sink. While I soaped the loofah, he pulled the shower curtain back and stepped into the shower. Before turning around to face Zy'Lon, I moved the showerhead up. As the water landed in the middle of his chiseled and dripped down his body, my mind was in a naughty place as I thought about us having sex in the shower as the water slammed into our connected bodies.

As I glared into his handsome face, I voiced in an authoritative timbre, "You already know what to do, sir."

"See, you spoilin' a nigga fo' real, Sexy Chocolate," he replied after licking his lips while moving closer to me.

With a smile on my face, I didn't say anything as I took my time washing his body. The loofah was in my right hand as I cleaned his left shoulder while my left hand massaged his right shoulder. I performed the same cleaning/massaging technique, and like always, I was halfway to his dick when Zy'Lon dropped his head back and exhaled. He was relaxed as I was in a world of my own, ensuring that he was relaxed as he figured things out concerning what he would do with the rest of his life.

For the past couple of days, I noticed that Zy'Lon was stressed. I wanted us to talk about it, but he didn't. I didn't like how uptight he could be in the middle of the night, so I ordered his ass to get in the shower. The only thing I knew that would relax a person was water and a set of comforting, soft hands. While I bathed his body, he opened up and talked to me. That night was the start of how I would get him to communicate with me freely.

"I'm tryin' to get up out of these streets, but I gotta know somethin', Sasha."

"What's that?" I questioned as I placed my eyes on him while I cleaned that lovely tool of his.

"What do you really want in a man? Do you see me as yo' man … possibly yo' husband one day?" he asked, placing his hazel-green, mesmerizing eyes on me.

Giving him my undivided attention, I honestly replied, "I want a man who respects, loves, and honors me. He'll move heaven and hell for me, gives me butterflies at the mention of his name or the slightest thought of him. I want a man who's all about me, wants to build a life with me, and can't go a day without talking or seeing me. A man who understands my complicated desires. A man who can satisfy me with his clothes on. Yes, I see you as my man, and, yes, I can see you as my husband."

"Even wit' my age, you see all that?"

I nodded my head as I said, "Yes."

"What if I say that I'm terrified of us gettin' close, an' then you decide that you can't handle the age difference?"

"What if I say that if you don't get that feeling and thought out of your mental, I will have to command Big Juke to whoop your ass?" I questioned in a joking manner.

Lightly chuckling, Zy'Lon glared at me with a look in his eyes that I had never encountered before from Charles or Marlon. Everything on my body tingled at the way I felt upon seeing the look of need in his beautiful eyes.

"Sasha, Charles told me 'bout you five years ago. The stuff that he said 'bout you had a young nigga fienin' to be in yo' presence. The way he described how you looked before he showed me a picture of you had a nigga searchin' low an' high fo' yo' ass. When he talked 'bout yo' character, outside of the submissive shit, I saw that glow in his eyes. He described a genuine, kind-hearted, thoughtful angel. That man worshipped the fuckin' ground you walked on causin' me to worship that ground too. Even though, you were a debt to him, he never acted nor talked like you were. He was the reason I fell in love wit' you. I didn't want any other female. I wanted what was in his presence … you. I kept my dick in condoms fo' a reason whenever I fucked a broad. I didn't get in any relationships fo' a reason. I wanted my first girlfriend to be you. If I was goin' to build wit' anybody … it was gonna be wit' you. I didn't know if I was up to par fo' you or not, but I had to see."

I didn't know what to say or how to feel. I just glared at him while biting my bottom lip. It seemed as if Charles was grooming Zy'Lon to be my man. At least, in a weird way, I hoped that's what he was doing.

"Talkin' time is over … fo' nih," he said before ordering me to hand him my wash cloth, so he could bathe me.

Doing as Zy'Lon requested, I didn't say a thing as I allowed him to clean every inch of me—minus my asshole. I wanted to clean that myself. Even though we didn't say a word, we were loud and clear— thanks to our actions towards one another. I couldn't lie like I wasn't mad at Charles for talking about me in the presence of another being, a being who worshipped me. Little did Zy'Lon know, in the short amount of time that we had been around each other, I was starting to worship the ground he walked on as well.

After our nice, quiet shower, we cleaned the tub and floor before placing clothes on our bodies. As we stepped into my room, I remembered that I didn't have any bananas for the banana pudding; thus, I told him that I had to take a trip to the store.

"What you forgot nih?" he asked as he placed his feet into a pair of all-white Jordan's.

"Bananas and Vanilla Wafers," I replied as I placed my eyes on his handsome self.

With a raised eyebrow and a serious facial expression, that fool said, "Mane, look, I just know you ain't tryin' to have Juke stay longer than I want his ass to. I don't feel like lookin' at that nigga eat up all the damn banana puddin'. We will become lil' churren in this bitch 'bout dat."

Laughing hard, I had to because I knew he was serious about them acting like little kids. It was in their nature to do so.

"Well, I don't know what to tell you because I want some banana pudding, so what are you going to do, Zy'Lon?" I asked sexily as I strolled towards him.

"I'm finna go get it," he huffed as the doorbell rang.

"That's probably him now," I stated as we ambled towards my front door together.

I was dead wrong about Big Juke being at my door; it was Marlon. Oh, the look on his face when he saw Zy'Lon standing behind me laughing before speaking.

"So, I guess you just gon' fuck an' leave her alone like you do all the other broads, huh, Big Nuke?"

"Mane, you can't ask me shit. Shouldn't you be doin' somethin' other than poppin' up over here?" Zy'Lon asked in a savage tone that turned me the fuck on.

"Y'all are not about to do this shit ... period," I spoke sternly as I pointed at them.

Of course, Marlon had to be the nigga who didn't hear shit I had to say.

"My nigga, she ain't gon' ever love you like she loves me, an' that's facts."

Chuckling, Zy'Lon replied, "I beg to differ, Marlon. I ain't finna argue wit' you, my nigga, but, um ... I ain't up fo' bein' disrespectful towards my lady, so I'mma let her handle you."

Before skipping out of my crib, Zy'Lon placed a kiss on my cheek before sternly saying, "Remember what I told you."

Nodding my head, I said, "Okay."

It was rare that Zy'Lon left me alone. Whenever he did, he made sure that I didn't open my door for anyone. Also, he made sure that if some shit popped off that I blasted whatever gun I was closest to and called him the moment I got a chance. I was thankful that I hadn't had to use any of the guns I had been trained to shoot yet.

"So, you an' this nigga shackin' up, Sasha?" Marlon asked.

Ignoring his question, I asked, "What did you come here for?"

"'Cause I want you in Marlia an' my lives. I want things to go back to the way that it was. I'm sorry fo' puttin' my hands on you. I'm sorry fo' blamin' you fo' Lil' Boo's death I can't imagine you not bein' in my life as my wife an' mother to my child ... hell, an' to our future kids," he announced sincerely as he gazed into my eyes.

Shaking my head as I focused on the wild black mane on his head, I said, "Marlon, I meant what I said when I left that note on the table at the hospital. I don't see myself being with you especially not after you beat me the way that you did. No, it wasn't right for me to slap you, and I apologize for that, but that still didn't give you the right to do what you did. I will never look at you the same for that very fact. Please, stop popping up at my home. Whatever we tried to have is long gone."

"So, you tellin' me that we are really done? Like done, done?"

"Yep. I just don't see myself being with you anymore. The moment you put your hands on me like that, followed by fucking me in such a disrespectful, rapist kind of way, you killed us."

"There's nothin' that I can do to make things up to you?" he asked softly while walking closer to me.

As I shook my head, I replied, "Not a thing, Marlon, not a thing."

He exited my home without a word or as much as a noise. Quickly, I closed and locked my door without a second thought. As I crossed the golden threshold of the kitchen, my doorbell rang. I knew it wouldn't be Zy'Lon because I had made him a key. Keeping in mind what he drilled into my head for days, I didn't make a noise as I grabbed the gun closest to the door.

Looking through my peephole, I bucked my eyes when I saw Myia with Big Juke. Knowing that it was safe for me to open the door, I did so.

"Ooou, you finna get in trouble," he said seriously before chuckling as he leaned in to hug me.

"What am I gonna get in trouble for?"

"'Cause you're not supposed to open the door ... even fo' me," he voiced as he saw Myia into my home before locking the door behind him.

"I know you won't hurt me or bring harm my way, so I highly doubt it if I'll get in trouble fo' that," I told him as I analyzed his body language.

"That ain't what the fuck I told yo' ass to do, Sasha! I said not to open that damn do' fo' no-damn-body. Ya' ass hardheaded as fuck. I bet yo' ass ain't gettin' not a damn tea or tablespoon of dick tonight. Yo' ass gon' learn to listen to me. I don't give a fuck if you is older than me! I said what the fuck I said!" Zy'Lon yelled from Big Juke's phone.

The moment Zy'Lon yelled that I wasn't getting a tea or tablespoon of dick tonight, Myia and Big Juke laughed until tears were rolling down their faces. I rolled my eyes at their asses before walking off mad as hell.

I bet I'ma get what the fuck I want.

"Let me get my ass off this phone, so I can buy the--," Zy'Lon said before cutting off his sentence only to say, "Mane, hell nawl, she ain't gettin' an ounce of this dick. Women so damn hardheaded it don't make no sense. I tell her ass not to do somethin', an' she do what she wanna."

"Nigga, who is you talkin' to?" Big Juke asked.

"Som' dude who was laughin' at what I said."

"Oh, well, hurry yo' ass up. Myia an' I eatin' over here tonight."

"Who an' who eatin' where?" Zy'Lon voiced curiously.

Chuckling, Big Juke said, "Act like ya' ass ain't heard me. Bring them damn 'nanas an' wafers on."

They started joking and talking shit as Myia took a seat next to me.

"Hey, do you need help in the kitchen or want us to purchase something for dinner?" she asked sweetly as I sighed and shook my head.

"No, we don't need anything, but I could always use your hands with this damn meatloaf. Only you can make it turn out just the way I like it," I smiled softly, placing my eyes on her.

"I love you, Sasha, and I didn't mean to hurt your feelings."

"You already know how I feel about you, Myia. I forgive you," I told her as that foolish negro, Big Juke, said aww.

"So, tell me how in the fuck did y'all end up at my door ... together?" I asked, looking at them.

"Now, that is a story fo' y'all to discuss while preparin' dinner, eh?"

Twenty minutes later, Myia and I were in the kitchen doing our thing as Big Juke and Zy'Lon were on the balcony smoking and talking. As Myia told me how she and Big Juke came to be "friends" as she kept telling me, I had a surprised facial expression. I was on the verge of asking her a question when we were interrupted by the fellas sternly looking at me. Immediately, I knew it was some shit.

"Myia, I'll be right back."

"Okay," she replied as I walked towards the balcony behind them.

Once I closed the door, they sighed heavily before Zy'Lon said, "Commander, we have a problem."

"And, what is that?" I asked in a calm voice.

With his eyes on me, Zy'Lon's tone was low as he said, "There's circulation goin' 'round that a possible hit order might be put out fo' Myia's uncle Henry an' yo' uncle Darrell ... the kicker part is if this shit is a fo' sho' hit ... we're the ones that gotta take them niggas out."

 Chapter 14

Marlon

Friday, May 25th

A nigga had been fucked up mentally ever since I left Sasha's crib Wednesday. She had a nigga's mind on wham as I thought about that nigga Big Nuke placing a kiss on her cheek. Never in a trillion years would I have thought that Sasha would shack up with a nigga like Big Nuke. That protection shit he told her I highly believed was a got damn lie. He just wanted to fuck because that was what type of nigga he was.

For three days, I tried to find a way to get rid of Big Nuke, but nothing I thought of was good enough. The only solution I came up with was to have him knocked off, but I didn't know who I was going to have do the deed for me. I didn't know many niggas who were willing to go up against Big Nuke and Big Juke. I had to cease my thoughts because I was having migraines out the ass while plotting to get rid of them niggas.

Myia was on some fuck shit. She was still talking to Big Juke. He was at her house, and they were spending unnecessary time together. I didn't like that shit one bit, and I let them know that shit too. Of course, Myia and I got into it. Big Juke sat on my sister's sofa as if he was a king with a smile on his face. One wrong comment out of Myia's mouth caused me to tell her some shit that I knew I was going to regret later. She was going to learn that she wasn't street, and that snakes come in all shapes and sizes.

Marlia was doing better. She was still in pain though. The medical team began scraping skin off small areas of her body. I couldn't stand the thought of how they were doing things to make my child's body somewhat okay. I couldn't imagine being in her shoes as she had to deal with another obstacle in her young life.

My mother and grandmother were by her side as Myia and I had to work. Every night, I would leave my job and head back to Birmingham. I didn't feel right not being by my daughter's side, but I was tired of being in that hospital room. There was something about hospitals that drained the fucking life out of you.

I would be glad when Marlia was in a better condition, so that we could blow the place. Since Quinn signed over her rights, I took the liberty of trying to upgrade to a two-bedroom apartment. We still had to go to family court to seal the deal, but like she promised, Quinn kept her word on not fucking with me or trying to fight me about the custody issue.

In a way, I was glad that Sasha used her power to make some of my life easier. She surely put Quinn and her mother in their place. I had to see for myself how fucked up Quinn's weak ass momma was. Boy, was she a fucked up sight. If I really cared for the woman, I would've felt bad for the lady, but I couldn't. She got what she deserved, and so did her stupid ass daughter.

Outside of planning for Sasha to be back in my life, knocking off Big Juke and Big Nuke, and arguing with Myia about being in another fuck nigga's company, I ordered Marlia's bedroom items—the theme was Hello Kitty. My daughter was so in love with that damn cat that I knew I had to cope it for her new bedroom. My mother, Myia, and my grandmother said that they would decorate her room to perfection, and I believed them.

"Shid, it looks like we finna get off early," one of my co-workers stated as we were at a standstill with loading trucks.

"We ain't got no work, huh?" I inquired as I looked around the hot warehouse.

"Nope. We just filled the last of the trucks fifteen minutes ago," he replied before our shift manager announced that there was no more work for us to do.

Happier than a motherfucker to be off at nine o'clock on a Friday night, I quickly walked off on the nigga who was standing beside me. I didn't have any plans of hitting the slab to Birmingham until the normal time when I got off—around two o'clock in the morning. So, I knew I had to have a little fun before heading back to my daughter.

"Aye, Marlon, what you finna get into?" a couple of the guys asked as I hopped off my forklift.

"These streets," I replied.

"Aye, you know Club G's be jumpin' 'round this time of the night," one of the guys stated happily.

"Well, that's the move then. I'm finna hit up my crib an' get fresh. I'll chop it up wit' y'all when I get there," I spoke loudly as I moved towards the clock-out machine.

Everyone was hustling and bustling to get out the warehouse. I didn't blame them. Like I said, it wasn't that often that we were off on Fridays, let alone be off before two o'clock in the morning.

After I clocked out, I was walking faster than a crackhead coming to cop some dope. Along the way to my vehicle, I overheard several people saying that they were going to Club G's. I knew I had to be in that joint too; I needed to let my hair down. A nigga had been through too much lately. I needed several drinks followed by the same amount of blunts. I wanted to feel somewhat normal again. If I didn't, I was going to lose my fucking mind.

As I unlocked my door, an innocent, soft voice asked, "Marlon, are you going to Club G's?"

"Yeah," I replied as I turned around and glared into the rounded face of a sexy, short, skinny, dark-brown broad.

"Cool. I'll see you there," she spoke while giving me the 'fuck me' eyes.

Chuckling, I replied, "A'ight. By the way, what's yo' name, shawty?"

"Dejah."

"A'ight, Dejah, I'll see ya' later."

"Okay," she happily responded with a smile on her face before walking off.

Taking a seat in my truck, I knew that I was going to dive deep into Dejah's pussy, so, she'd better get ready.

A nigga had too much pressure and stress flowing through his body, and I had to find a bitch to take it out on. Sasha would've gotten all this pressure, but she was too busy underneath Big Nuke's ass.

As I zipped away from my job, I was super amped as Yo Gotti's song "Look in the Mirror" blasted from my woofers. In the mood to beat down the block, I did that the moment I turned the volume up on the radio. Bopping and weaving in and out of traffic crunk as fuck in the front seat while firing up a blunt, I was too eager to see some ass and titties bouncing. I was ready to have bitches staring and asking to come home with me. I was in need of feeling myself again. What other way to get my head swollen other than by being around a bunch of thirsty yet sexy ass bitches?

Fifteen minutes later, I was pulling into the parking lot in front of my apartment door. After I shut off my engine, I hopped out of my truck with my phone in my hand. A few steps away from my door, I dialed Trandall's number. On the second ring, he answered.

"What's up?" I quickly asked.

"Shit. Finna hit up Club G's. How's work?" he asked while inhaling, what I knew was a blunt.

"Finna get dressed an' hit that club up as well," I told him as I unlocked the door.

"Oh, shit. The turn up finna be real!" he loudly spat before chuckling.

"On life, it is. You comin' by here or what?" I questioned as I stepped into my cool home.

"Yeah. You drivin' or not?"

"Yeah, I'm drivin', but once I fuck som' I'mma head up to Birmingham."

"A'ight. I'll be at yo' crib in a minute."

"A'ight. Use yo' key. I'll probably be in the shower."

"Bet."

"Bet."

The moment I ended the call, I ran to my room. There wasn't a need for me to figure out what I was going to wear. I had newly bought clothes and shoes that I hadn't worn yet. I knew for a fact that I wanted to wear black and green, and my jewelry selection was going to be gold of course. I had a pair of gold glasses that I was going to have strap tight on my face. They weren't prescription glasses, just some shit to stunt in; the bitches loved seeing me in glasses.

Stripping out of my clothes, Sasha crossed my mind again. I had the urge to call her, but I refrained from doing so. Heading towards the shower, I heard my front door open followed by Trandall making an announcement that he was going to raid my refrigerator for something to drink.

"A'ight!" I yelled as I walked into my bathroom.

An hour later, I was standing in front of my dresser mirror checking out my appearance. My black jeans had the perfect crease, and the customized green, gold, and black belt I wore popped my outfit off. My black, collared, Ralph Lauren shirt was wrinkle free. My barely worn, all-black with a small section of green, Jordan's were clean. I didn't do shit with my wavy black hair. I had that shit looking wild as fuck. A gold watch was slapped onto my right wrist, and two gold pinky rings were secured on my long fingers. A nice-sized gold chain was loosely hanging around my neck, and the golds in my mouth were shining hard as fuck. My favorite cologne was sprayed evenly on my body. I made sure to have some on my neck. I wanted to make the bitches' pussies wet the moment they placed their mouth to my ear.

"Got damn, nigga. An hour, an' you still ain't ready?" Trandall asked in an annoyed tone.

"Nigga, I'm ready. I had to make sure that I'm all the way fly as fuck."

"Dude, bring yo' ass on. Shit," Trandall voiced as I continued to make sure that I was on point.

Nodding my head, I left my room satisfied with the way that I looked.

"Aye, mane, I heard that nigga Big Nuke shackin' up wit' Sasha."

I didn't want to have my mood ruined by the talks of them; thus, I said, "Mane, I righteously don't want to hear shit 'bout them. I just want to have a fun night. I'll deal wit' that shit later."

"Marlon, what the fuck do you mean you will deal wit' that shit later?" Trandall questioned as I placed my hand on the doorknob.

"Just what the fuck I said. Them niggas ain't good enough fo' them."

"Whoa. Whoa. What do you know?" Trandall questioned seriously.

"Myia an' Big Juke conversin' a lot nih. I went over to Sasha's a couple of days ago, an' that nigga Big Nuke made it clear that him an' Sasha got mo' goin' on than him protectin' her. Let's just say that I refuse to have them niggas corrupt or put Sasha and Myia into som' shit they ain't got no business bein' in."

"An' how are you goin' to do that?"

"Have them knocked off."

With a shocked facial expression, Trandall asked lowly, "Do you really hear what the fuck you are sayin'?"

"Yep."

"Mane, you need to rethink that shit."

"Them niggas ain't finna fuck them over. Sasha only wit' the nigga 'cause her self-esteem fucked up right now. She vulnerable an' I will not let Big Nuke take advantage of her."

"Dude, you trippin'. You be doin' the fuckin' most, man. Let them girls live their lives. Last time we stepped into som' shit, Lil' Boo died. Mane, chill out on that knockin' off shit. Ain't no tellin' who in the fuck will get hurt this time."

Seeing that Trandall wasn't feeling what I was talking about, I lied to him as if I wasn't going to do anything, but he didn't know that I was going to be scouting for potential shooters soon. I was bound to find someone who would be willing to knock those niggas off. They weren't as well-loved as everyone thought; that was for damn sure. There wasn't a dope boy in the country that was loved by everybody; there was always a hater lurking somewhere trying to get a chance to knock a hot dope nigga off his throne.

I just had to find the right one who was going to blow the powerful cousin's eyes out of their sockets!

Zy'Lon

"So, you really thinkin' heavy 'bout leavin' the streets, huh?" Juke asked as he strolled out on to the balcony.

"I don't see why not. I got mad money. A nigga ain't hurtin' fo' shit fo' real. So why continue this lifestyle when I ain't hungry or homeless?" I told him as I looked at him.

"True, true … honestly, I ain't have to worry 'bout the shit that you had too. So I guess this lifestyle is entertainin' fun fo' me. I guess I just don't wanna give up the easy money," he sighed while firing up a blunt.

As I nodded my head, I gulped down the rest of the V8 Splash Tropical Blend. Sitting back in a lounge chair, I observed the calm, humid night. The dark sky was highlighted by millions of brightly shining stars. The wind was minimal as the heat stuck to a nigga's skin worse than maggots sticking to a corpse. Crickets and other ugly bugs did their fuck calls or whatever they had going on. Shit, they were making unnecessary fucking noise, put it that way.

"Just wonderin'," Juke quickly said, interrupting my thoughts.

"Yeah," I voiced as I looked his way.

"You gon' leave this lifestyle behind fo' Sasha?"

"I been wantin' to leave it alone, but you weren't ready … so I had to stick by you. But, now, that she's semi-pressin' the issue, an' I think it's time fo' us to leave this shit behind. Why not go an' create a family or at least travel without bein' on a mission? I'm ready fo' the life I've been wantin' before that mother of mine became a crackhead."

Nodding his head, Juke said, "I feel ya' … well, a little bit."

"You wouldn't leave the streets behind fo' Myia?" I inquired as I heard the women cackling, which was a good sight.

"Nope."

"Are you serious?"

"Yep. If she know that I love this lifestyle, then she would have to adapt to *my* world. The only reason I'm gettin' out is 'cause you want out, not 'cause of no broad."

Shaking my head, I said, "I fucked you up. Now, I hate that I introduced you to this part of the world. You had a good thing goin' wit' school an' shit. I did too, but hell ... I was a fuckin' kid bum wit' nobody to care fo' me. Jy'Lon, I'm sorry I brought you into this shit. Now, that I want out, I know it's got you feelin' some type of way."

"Honestly, I knew one day that you were goin' to gather enough money to go legit. I just didn't think it would be this soon. Like twenty-two type of soon. I thought we had at least fo' mo' years under our belt before we called it quits. An' there is no need in apologizin' to me, man. It ain't like you put a gun to my head. I willingly agreed. Hell, I've been in love wit' money ever since I saw my dad pull out a wad of cash an' seein' him move all that work. It was bound to happen anyway."

"Maybe not," I responded as the Sasha and Myia started singing, fucking up somebody's song.

As we looked at the ladies, Juke said, "She didn't say a word 'bout us knockin' her uncle off. I wonder why?"

"One thing I've learned 'bout Sasha is if you're on her bad side, yo' ass will stay there. It's apparent that her uncle did somethin' that pissed her off, but that Henry nigga had her a little stuck," I said as my cellphone rang.

Looking at Johnnie's number, I said, "I wonder what in the fuck he finna say."

"Must be Johnnie."

"Yep," I replied before answering my phone.

As I told Johnnie to speak to me, I placed the phone on speaker while Juke squatted beside me. I ensured that the volume of the speaker was turned down enough, so we would be the only ones able to hear the message.

"Where is Sasha?" Johnnie spoke in a raspy timbre.

"In the house. What's up?" I inquired as I looked through the clean balcony window at the beautiful creature dancing and having fun with Myia.

"I called her phone. She's not answerin'."

"What do you need, Johnnie?"

"I need to speak wit' Sasha. She's the commander. She needs to be fully involved wit' what I'm 'bout to say. Honestly, I only need to speak wit' her."

As I cleared my throat, I had the need to curse Johnnie's ass out, but I knew I didn't have a place at the moment. Sasha was the commander after all, and I had to respect the game.

Juke opened the sliding door and told Sasha to come here. Myia was in tow when he shook his head at her and said, "Sasha is the only one needed."

"Fellas, I hope we don't have anything important to discuss," Sasha voiced sternly as she looked between Juke and me.

"I'm afraid so," we replied in unison.

Sighing heavily, she lowly said, "What kind of business?"

"Come take a seat in my lap," I told her before Johnnie spoke to her.

"Hey, Johnnie, how are you?" she inquired while placing her head on my chest, hair all in a nigga's face, which I loved.

"I'm good. There's an order out, and the exact execution on how things must go down needs to be discussed first thing in the morning. Those invested in the matter will be in town tomorrow morning around fo' o'clock. They want to discuss things promptly at six o'clock in the morning. The location is the same as always. I'm sure you have been told where those meetings and things take place. Correct?"

As she nodded her head, she said, "Yes."

"Okay. Have you thought of the execution plan?"

"No, I haven't. I need more details into one of those beings. The other I couldn't careless to know the details," she spoke in a tone that had my dick poking her in the ass.

She finna get off punishment early, if she keep on talkin' like this.

"Um, what kind of details do you need, and on which one?" Johnnie questioned in a curious, impatient tone.

"Henry."

"There isn't much information on him. The investors just want that taken care of," he spat.

"Well, I tell you what," she stated quickly before lightly chuckling, "You and those damn investors get me the fucking information I want, and if the shit is deemed plausible, then I will grant it. If it's not, then y'all better get the fuck out of my face with that nonsense. Oh, and by the way, from here on out, make sure that y'all provide me with evidence before having an order placed. Understood?"

Oh, yeah, she finna get all this dick tonight.

"Yes, ma'am."

"Is there anything else you would like to discuss?"

"No, ma'am."

"I will not be up at the crack of dawn for a fucking meeting, so it's in your best interest and everyone else's to have that damn time changed to noon. Understood?"

Shittt, she got me mad as hell an' intrigued at the same time. I need me som' of her ret nih.

"Yes, ma'am."

"Very well then, now, have a great night."

"You as well, ma'am," Johnnie spoke before the call ended.

Juke and I looked at Sasha with blank facial expressions. If I was in awe, I knew that he was as well. Charles didn't command like Sasha did. He went along with whatever the investors said without so much as questioning shit that was said. Sasha had to see the reasons of having someone knocked off. Against my better judgment, that wouldn't be something that I would do. Getting too personal with an individual would cause problems for everyone involved.

Rolling her thin neck from side-to-side, Sasha said, "Whenever I do turn things over to someone else, it will be Johnnie, and you two will *not* be under his wing. He has a sey way of doing things ... I guess Charles must've trained him that way. However, I will not have you two be a part of this shit. With that being said, y'all better get ready to transition out. The longer y'all pussyfoot around, the longer I will be commander. Understood?"

Juke nodded his head as I sighed heavily all the while shaking mine. I swear I hated that Johnnie's dumb ass had the nerve to tell her about her position. I wasn't going to tell her shit because she didn't need to be in this lifestyle either. She was starting to become too comfortable, and I knew that I couldn't get out with the snap of my fingers. I had to slowly get out. There were plenty of people I had to talk to in order for them to trust that I would keep my fucking mouth shut.

"Well, no more business talk. Myia and I want to go out. Sooo ... are we hitting up a club or not?" she asked in her normal tone.

"I ain't up fo' no clubbin', Sasha," I spoke as Juke told her that he was all for going out.

I was outnumbered, and guess who was royally pissed the fuck off? I hated being in clubs. It was too packed, and I couldn't enjoy myself because I had to watch out for niggas and bitches who might try some slick shit.

Myia's ass had to go home and get some clothes; Juke stayed behind. While he was in the guest bathroom handling his business, I was in the master bathroom. I tried to get Sasha to get in with me, but she wasn't having it. She was hell bent on going out; whereas, I was hell bent on doing some other things that didn't require us to be in a building filled with musty ass folks who I didn't want staring in my face.

Two-and-a-half-hours later, we were ready to hit the club scene. Juke had some crazy shit to say about Myia's ensemble. She wasn't dressed half-naked or anything; she was dressed and shaped just like Sasha, stacked in all the right places.

"I know damn well you don't think you wearin' that out, Myia. You might as well get ready to change into somethin' else," he spat seriously while ogling Myia.

"Nigga, I'm not finna change my clothes. There is nothing wrong with what I have on," she said, laughing.

As they went back and forth about the red crop top shirt, white high-rise shorts, and red closed-toe stiletto heels, my mouth watered as Sasha had me hypnotized. She wore the hell out of her outfit—a bronze- hued crop top shirt, black high-rise shorts, and closed-toe bronze colored heels. My baby's body was glistening. Her favorite sweet-scented perfume was sprayed evenly throughout her attire, and her bushy mane was tamed to perfection. The top was placed in a loose ponytail as the back hung down, and a small tendril hung on each side by her ears. Her choice of jewelry color was all gold. She wasn't big on makeup, but she had her eyebrows and eyelids lightly made up, and those juicy ass lips shined with a double coat of lip gloss.

"You heard what I said," Juke loudly spoke as I held out my hand for Sasha to place her slim hand in.

"Sasha, use that voice that makes them calm down," Myia joked, causing us to laugh.

"Oou, you dead as wrong fo' that." Juke laughed as he nodded his head.

"Can we leave now?" Sasha asked in the most innocent voice ever.

"Not until Myia change clothes," he spoke sternly.

Sasha looked at Myia with a smile on her face before looking at Juke and then me.

"I said I am ready to go," she said in that sexy-ass commander tone.

"Fuckkk!" Juke spat, causing us to laugh again as we moved towards the door.

"On life, Myia, when we leave this club ... yo' ass is in so much fuckin' trouble. You wrong fo' havin' her pull out that hat," Juke said in a not-so-pleased tone.

"Look at it this way, Jy'Lon," Myia quickly stated in a seductive voice, "You get to see me in my natural habitat before climbing in between my enchanting jungle."

Sasha and Myia burst out laughing as I locked and closed the door behind me. With a quizzical look on his face, Juke opened his mouth to say something as he looked at me. I just shook my head as I didn't know what the hell she meant, and I sure as hell wasn't going to ask.

The ride to the club was enjoyable and funny as fuck. While sitting in the backseat of my truck, Myia and Juke playfully argued and disagreed about everything. It was cool seeing him out of his element. He talked that shit earlier like a female wouldn't make him leave the streets, but he was a bold face liar. Sasha said what she wanted out of us, and he didn't protest. True enough, what she said goes; however, he could have politely contested against it. My cousin was feeling Myia more than he said.

Juke had been in more relationships than any older nigga. He used broads for different reasons, and love was nowhere in his plans for them. Within two days of them being in his presence, he had them doing all types of illegal shit for him. Whereas, Myia had been in his presence longer and not one time did he mention her doing some illegal shit on his behalf.

"Damn, this bitch is stupid blowed," Myia stated in awe.

I'm ready to go back to the crib, I thought as I didn't see a place to park.

"Damn, they got Hardee's on lock," Sasha stated as I whipped into the blocked restaurant.

In front of me was a sign about paying to park in the restaurant's parking lot. Rolling down the window, I handed the chunky security guard a crisp ten-dollar bill.

"They so damn schemed out in this city," Juke laughed as the man waved me through the homemade gate filled with orange cones.

After I parked, I took my gun off me, but I made sure that a round was in the head. I didn't have to tell Juke to make sure that his shit was locked and loaded. He knew what we were up against—quite a few niggas and bitches that were always on the lookout for a come up.

As we stepped out of my whip, eyes landed on us. A few niggas that I knew strolled towards me, and we quickly dapped and chopped it up. The sight of niggas who didn't say shit to me, yet, had their eyes on what was meant for me had a nigga smiling.

As my baby noticed that they were ogling her, Sasha's thick, sexy ass cut the light conversation the niggas and I had by one lone word, "Baby."

"I'mma holla at y'all later," I told them before I ambled towards her as she stood ever so sexily with a look on her face that had me ready to put her ass back in the passenger's seat and drive off.

Ten minutes later, we were inside of the semi-cool, packed club. The layout of the club was nothing spectacular, but it wasn't rundown either. There was a nice space within the used-to-be restaurant. The vibe of those in my space was cool. People laughed, talked, and bobbed their heads along to one of Young Jeezy's songs. Cigarette and Black and Mild smoke were heavy in the air as well as cologne and perfume. Like any club that's heavily populated with Black folks, there were half-naked bitches. They had niggas and bitches' attention. There were casually dressed individuals in the club as well.

Myia and Sasha stopped at the bar. I shook my head as I wrapped my hands around Sasha's waist. She felt absolutely amazing in my arms. With a harden dick, I lightly pressed my tool into her juicy, jiggly behind, causing her to turn her head and mouth for me to behave.

Dropping my mouth to her ear, I whispered, "Make me."

Shaking her head with a smirk on her face, she faced forward. I wanted her ass to say something smart; she would've been out the club within nine nanoseconds.

Not feeling the line to the bar, Juke made his presence known when he saw a couple of niggas who moved dope for us in the city. The moment those characters knew we were in the building, they told us to come up. Neither of the women nor I moved, just Juke. He knew to get a variety of shit to drink, bottles only. We didn't do that cup shit.

"It's in my car, it's in my clothes, that make these hoes fuck fo' sho!" Webbie's voice blasted from the loud speakers within the club, causing Myia, Sasha, and I to bob our heads as we rapped along with the song.

Out of us three, Sasha was the crunkest one. One thing I had learned about that woman was that she loved her rap songs, and that was alright in my book. I thought I would've been the one vibing hard to the song, but I was dead wrong. Sasha took over to the point she had motherfuckers at the bar glaring at her.

The moment Juke waltzed towards us with three pails of Corona's, a small cup of lemons and limes, two bottles of Moscato, and two bottles of Hennessy, we sauntered away from the bar. We had enough shit to drink for the duration of our stay, just the way I planned for it to be.

We decided to sit closest to the dance floor. There was a table free of debris and people. I was surprised to see that a club this packed didn't have anyone sitting at the table. Instantly, I became skeptical of shit; however, Juke took it upon himself to claim the table as ours.

As he placed the pails on the table, we pulled out the chairs for the ladies. They opened their bottles and took a nice swig before releasing the rim from their glossy lips. They were on the verge of sitting down; that was until a beat dropped that had the fucking club on fire—mostly by the women. I had the pleasure of hearing the unknown name of the song from a group of niggas named Orgy Boyz. One thing I knew about the song was that bitches were going to show their natural asses.

"Look at dat ass, look at dat ass, look at dat ass, on dat bitch," blasted from the speakers, prompting Myia and Sasha to sashay away from the table with their tongues out of their mouths as they bounced their asses.

Juke and I knew they were going to show out. There were no ifs, ands, or buts about it, so we had to be prepared for some no-manner-having niggas trying to step to behind them. I was going to shut the fucking club down about mine.

Those got damn women turned around, gazed at us, and danced just for us. My eyes were logged on Sasha as she dropped all that ass to the ground, leaned back, and rocked her hips from left to right. Slowly coming forward, she had ass bouncing for days.

"Mane, I'mma fuck Myia ass up the moment we make it some-fuckin-where. Milawd, cus, I ain't know she could throw an' pop that pussy like that. Shatt!" Juke loudly spat in my ear in pure awe.

"If you want this money hoe, you gotta shake some," Sasha mouthed as she looked at me with a wicked facial expression.

A young nigga gon' fuck yo' ass som' good tonight. On my crackheaded-ass momma, I'mma fuck yo' ass good, I thought as Sasha brought the bottle of Hennessy to her lips.

The way she danced imitated the way she pussy popped and rode my dick some nights ago. In a flash, I was standing behind her thick ass.

"Ass an' titties, ass an' titties, ass an' titties!" the crowd shouted along with the rappers.

Sasha had a nigga's dick on brick mode by the time she bust a split on the floor. Money flew towards her as niggas gathered to see her dance. Not liking that shit at all, I snatched her up.

Angrily, I placed my mouth to her ear and said, "Don't fuckin' play wit' me, Sasha. You ain't no damn hoe. Don't do no shit like that no fuckin' mo'. I'll shut this bitch down."

As I took a seat, I placed her on my lap. Juke followed suit and had Myia sitting on his lap. Myia and Sasha had something concocted because they kept looking at each other with a wicked smile all the while bobbing their heads and rolling their bodies to another song by Orgy Boyz.

"It's time to fuck ... what's up, what's up!" the rappers spat from the speakers.

All into the song, those damn women had eyes logged onto our table. I didn't like that type of attention. I couldn't fully watch my surroundings with Sasha dancing nastily in front of me. She threw her ass in my face, and I sure as fuck didn't waste any time biting those juicy cheeks of hers. When the song came to an end, I was ready to go and do just what the song said—fuck. Not pressing the issue about leaving, I sat back and let the ladies have fun while Juke and I chopped it up.

An hour later, Sasha sat on my lap and faced me. The look in her eyes told me that she wanted daddy to slide off in her. Signaling for Juke to wrap things up, I couldn't wait to get her out of the club and into her bedroom.

Sasha placed her mouth to my ear and sexily cooed, "I want you inside of me ... neow."

"Oh, we finna go," I told her.

"No, we ain't."

"What you mean?" I asked quickly before gazing into her beautiful, glistening face.

"I want you inside of me in this club. I found a ducked off spot by DJ booth. It's completely dark. I have a black satin strap in my shorts' pocket. Zy'Lon, I want you to tie my wrists up and fuck me against the wall. When we make it back to my ... well, *our* place, I *need* you to be my Dom ... just for the night," she whimpered in my ear as she sneakily hunched me.

Wait. What? What in the fuck am I supposed to do as her Dom? Charles ain't give me no fuckin' instructions on that shit. Hell, he didn't say anythin' 'bout it.

Since I had been fucking, I never had the urge to fuck in the club. The car, hell yes, but the club was a no-no. The look in my baby's eyes told me that I had to get on board with a lot of freaky shit that she liked to do. So, what did a nigga like me do? I told her ass to lead the fucking way. Apparently, the DJ read my girl's mind because he played "You" by Plies featuring Tank.

"You thinkin' 'bout me, suckin' on you, you suckin' on me," I sang along to one of the hottest sex songs ever made.

Seeing that there were quite a few people in our way, Sasha did the unthinkable—she faced me and slow danced. As I had my hands on the small of her back, she slowly backed us into the dark area where there was no one. Deep in the dark, no one could see us as she began rubbing on my swollen dick. Remembering what she said about a satin tie in her back pocket, I tied that motherfucker tight around her wrists as I bumped her ass against the wall.

We couldn't see each other, but I imagined the delightful look in her eyes. Roughly, I pulled her hands above her head. I felt her unsteady breaths against my chest. With her hands tied, I brought them over my head.

Placing my mouth to her ear, I asked, "Is this what you want, baby?"

"Yesssss," she cooed, damn near making me weak.

Not in the mood to rush anything with her, I unzipped her shorts. Once they were around her ankles I ordered for her to kick them off. Shit took off the moment I began toying with her steaming, wet pussy and her small bud. From the way she scratched my neck and tighten her pussy muscles, I knew that she was enjoying my skillful fingers.

Pushing my head with her thin wrists, Sasha indicated that she wanted my head close to hers. With the tip of my tongue hanging out, I was eager to taunt Sasha with my pink, long, and wide flesh. As I licked and sucked on her bottom lip, I worked my fingers so well inside of her super soaker that her legs shook uncontrollably. Engaging in a sensual kiss, Sasha took the lead and had a nigga in a zone I never wanted to leave. Not wanting to stop the finger play, I didn't. That was until it seemed like Sasha snatched skin from the back of my neck as her mouth slipped away from mine.

Big Sean featuring Kash Doll's song "So Good" blasted through the speakers, amping my ass up even more. I was on another level as I could absolutely relate to what Big Sean had to say about a woman with great head and pussy. Ready to dive inside of Sasha as she was pinned up against the wall, I unzipped my pants. As I rubbed the head of my dick against her wet, starving monkey, Sasha was panting and begging for me to stick him inside of her.

When I did, I had to say Big Sean's hook in her ear. My forehead rested on her forehead as I slowly grinded inside of her. Thrust for thrust, stroke for stroke, Sasha met every fucking one I threw at her. She twirled her body to the right, and I swerved my dick in the opposite direction. I ensured that I hit every spot that would have her pussy leaking and wanting more. I left not one corner of her dripping twat untouched.

"Fuck me from the back," she whimpered with her hands pressed tightly against the back of my head.

Once I removed her hands from around my neck and helped her to stand erect, I bent low. With her leg in the air, I feasted on the place that I had dreamed of kissing and licking on since Charles told me about her. From the way that she gripped the back of my head and the sudden change in her position, I knew her back was arched—she was about to cum. Eager to receive all the nutrients that my body needed, I ate her ass out while trap music blasted throughout the club.

After she blessed my throat and stomach with her minerals and vitamins, I gave her ass the best fuck from the back she ever received. I wanted it nice with a touch of rough; Sasha wanted it rough with a touch of nasty. Understanding what she wanted, I gave it to her ass—raw and uncut.

My phone vibrated, and I ignored the hell out of it. I was pleasing my lady. I had to pray that no shit was about to go down as I was in the corner satisfying the future Mrs. Zy'Lon Greggory.

Webbie's "Give Me That" played, and I lost my fucking mind as I felt Sasha's guts, soaking wet and tight. In the dark, I wore Sasha out while she had her ass up in the air and her hands around her ankles. I knew she was loudly moaning, cooing, and begging for more, so I gave her just what *I* needed her to have.

Her pussy muscles started to contract, and I really lost my fucking mind. I smacked her ass and yelled, "Give me dat pussy, guh!"

I knew she couldn't hear me, but if she knew me like I thought she did, she knew exactly where my mind was at while the song was playing. By the end of the song, Sasha was full of nut, and I was sweating like a motherfucker in Egypt.

Pulling up my pants with my right hand, I held onto my baby. Once we got ourselves together, we sneakily exited the dark area we had blessed with our little spontaneous sex session. As we held our heads high while slow dancing into the spotlight, I scanned the area to see what the vibe was like. It was the same as it was when we entered the secret fuck spot—motherfuckers dancing, smoking, drinking, and having a good time.

Halfway towards the table where Myia and Juke were slow dancing, a sight caught my eyes that made me stop in my track. Sasha asked me what was wrong, but I couldn't say shit as I saw Marlon dancing with someone he had no business dancing with. If I was a dirty ass nigga, I would've never said a bitch ass thing, but I couldn't let the nigga go out like that.

"Aye, you might want to go an' tell that nigga Marlon … that's a tranny he dancin' an' gropin' on." I chuckled in Sasha's ear.

Instantly, she dropped my hand and walked over to the nigga who had it bad for my girl. She was inches away from me when Myia stopped slow dancing with Juke. As Myia moved towards Sasha, the tranny, and Marlon, Sasha whispered into Marlon's ear. The look on that nigga's face had me laughing like a motherfucker. I was beyond tickled. Strolling towards Juke, I shook my head as he looked at me confused.

"Mane, where in the fuck you been? Why they over there?" Juke impatiently asked as I turned to look at the scene that was unfolding.

Ignoring his first question, I said, "I told Sasha that she needed to tell Marlon that he was dancin' an' gropin' on a tranny."

"Yeah, I saw that shit," Juke laughed.

"Wow. Why you ain't tell Myia?" I asked with a smile on my face.

"Fuck that nigga. He tryin' to come between me an' his sister."

Chuckling, I replied, "Cusm you really ain't shit."

"Especially if you ain't on my good side."

As we looked at the somewhat calm scene, I could tell that Marlon was highly embarrassed and wanted to do something to the tranny from Tuscaloosa, but he didn't. I'm sure that Myia and Sasha told him about the charges he would get for putting his hands on someone of that nature, so he stormed off.

When he bypassed us, Juke was laughing his ass off, causing Marlon hit a U-turn and come our way. Sighing deeply, I had to get ready for the shit. At the end of the day, I was going to have my cousin's back, like he always had mine. Myia and Sasha intervened before Juke got real ignorant in the club, which was going to make me go postal.

They talked some sense into Marlon, so he left one pissed off nigga. As I watched him walked passed the bar, he scooped up a short, brown-skinned broad. Shaking my head, I placed my attention on my lady as she had an odd facial expression plastered across her beautiful face. The moment I made one got damn step towards Sasha, all hell broke loose. Bottles and shit were being broken on folks' head, and motherfuckers were throwing tables, chairs, and beer bottles.

Not the type of nigga to be in a chaotic scene, I yoked Sasha up iton my arm as Juke did the same to Myia. Bow guarding our way through the crowd, I saw that I had to take extreme measures to ensure that we got out of the 'one way in, one way out' type of establishment. Seeing the cluster fuck, I became pissed off as folks didn't move out of my way fast enough. Tired of the fuckery, Juke and I started shoving people out of the way. At the sight of our dope pushers, they whipped out their tools—making it easy for us and them to get out of the club.

Shit, why in the fuck didn't I think to call these niggas up, so I would be allowed to bring a pistol in the club?

Once we were safe, I was one mad motherfucker. Juke and I thanked the niggas that came through on a huge tip. To show our gratitude, we gave them a sweet offer they couldn't refuse as each of them showed their gold grills.

"We ain't comin' back to this motherfuckin' place no damn mo'!" I yelled as I reversed my truck from the parking spot.

"Not even for our secret spot?" Sasha asked sexily while glaring at me.

My attitude changed drastically upon the mention of the dark fucking area.

"What secret spot, bitch?" Myia inquired, curiously.

We didn't say a word as Myia repeated herself. Rapidly leaving the scene, Sasha was throwing subliminal messages, causing me to blush and shit.

"Yo' ass got a lot of mouth right now. Let's see how well that mouth gon' move some' when we get back home." I shot back while taking a brief glance at her.

"Ooou, Zaddy Zy'Lon, you know how this mouth move," she cooed in that damn commander's tone.

Oh, my fuckin' god! I swear I'm glad she knocked that nigga Charles off.

Chapter 16
Marlon

Sunday, May 27th

My mental hadn't been right ever since I left the club Friday night. After I learned the true nature of the motherfucker I was rubbing and touching on, I wanted to fuck that nasty, sick individual up. That motherfucker Big Juke had the audacity to laugh. I felt like he knew what I was up against but didn't tell my sister shit. Thus, I was glad when my plans of having him and that fuck nigga Big Nuke knocked the fuck off would take place.

Before shit popped off with the tranny issue, I overheard some niggas who wanted to set shit off with the powerful cousins, but they saw a group of niggas that had permission to carry their guns inside the club. Those same niggas fucked with Big Juke and Big Nuke heavy; it would be a bloodbath in the club if they capped off. Plus, I didn't want my sister and Sasha in the middle of harm's way. I had to scope out the area before I told the niggas where they could find those niggas. The moment I got the chance, I approached them. Like the ducks they were, they ate up the information I gave them.

After I snatched up the bitch that I worked with, we exited the building with a smile on our faces. She was smiling because she was going to get dicked down by me, and I was smiling because the powerful cousins were going to lose their lives. I was going to be in the front row to see them die; their bodies were going to be riddled with bullets, just like I had requested.

"Mmm, good morning," Dejah happily voiced as she opened her eyes.

"Moanin'," I replied, looking at the time on my phone. It read eleven thirty a.m.

"You were amazing last night, better than I thought you'd be," she cooed as she began rubbing on my dick.

I did what I needed to do; there was no need in her thinking she was going to milk me fucking dry. She wasn't Sasha. She couldn't get the dick like that.

"What you doin' fo' the day?" I asked with a raised eyebrow, a clear indication that I wanted her out of my face.

"Nothing. What's up?" she asked with a smile on her pretty face, clearly not getting the hint.

"Shid, finna link up wit' my fam later on, but, um … I got som' shit I need to take care of."

"Oh. Okay," she replied in a disappointed tone.

As I stood, she said, "How were things for you … meaning the sex between us?"

Taken aback by that weird question, I asked, "Are you askin' me how was the sex between us?"

Nodding her head as she lowly replied, "Yes."

I burst out laughing before I knew it, shaking my head as I continued to laugh. Apparently, she didn't know the number one rule of not asking a nigga how the sex was. Never had I ever had a bitch ask me a dumbass question like that.

"Why are you laughing, Marlon?"

Shaking my head, I said, "Mane, get dressed so that I can handle my business."

"Why are you being so nasty?" she probed as she lifted the covers off of her pretty naked body.

Ignoring her question, I asked, "Can you be ready to go in five minutes?"

She didn't say a word as she quickly dressed. She didn't bother putting her shoes on; she just snatched them off the floor, followed by grabbing her cellphone and keys. Not a single word left her mouth as she exited my bedroom. Once she was out of my crib, I sighed heavily as I locked my door.

I didn't have anything planned; I just didn't want to be bothered with her ass. Dejah had some good pussy, and her head game was a'ight, but she wasn't nothing like my Sasha. So, there was no need in keeping her around.

For four hours, I chilled at the house. I called my mother and checked on Marlia. She was sleeping. I made sure to inform my mother that I would be back in Birmingham once I rested. I lied to her like I had a headache from last night, and that was my reason for not coming to the hospital. I wouldn't dare tell my mother the real reason why I didn't come to the hospital. I wasn't even worried about Trandall or Myia saying that I was there.

Ring. Ring. Ring.

Looking at my phone, I saw Trandall's name. On the third ring, I answered.

"Yo'," I voiced.

"Mane, where in the hell did you duck off to last night?" he asked, inhaling.

I sure as hell wasn't going to tell his ass that I was secluded in a corner with a fucking tranny, so I did what most niggas would've done in my situation—lied.

"Mane, I was in the back of the club gettin' my dick sucked. That lil' slim shawty, Dejah, that I hugged when I strolled in the club."

"Oouuwee, that's one bad ass, short bitch there. I know you gon' keep her on yo' team."

"Nawl, I want Sasha's ass."

For thirty minutes, we went back and forth about Sasha and me. That nigga got the best of me when he brought up the fact that she and Zy'Lon were in the darkest area of the club. Instantly, I knew where he was talking about. That part of the club I had dicked down plenty of bitches and got my dick sucked.

Feeling myself about to say some shit, I halted my original words—in need of changing the subject.

"You goin' to Ms. Suelle's house today?"

"She must be doin' another cookout?" Trandall's greedy ass asked.

"Yep."

"Shid, I would love to, but you know how Sasha feels 'bout us."

"Her an' Myia was in the club togetha nigga ... even though they were wit' them niggas. You know Sasha ain't mad at us no mo'."

"Nawl, I ain't tryin' to be in her space like that. She's mo' powerful than you think she is."

"She won't let anythin' happen to us, an' you know it. Bro, come wit' me. I haven't had no good cookin' sense Marlia been up in that damn hospital."

"Speakin' of Marlia, how she's doin'?"

"Bring yo' ass up there an' see yo' lil' cousin. Then, you'll know."

"A'ight. You headin' back up there today?"

"Yeah, after I leave Ms. Suelle's crib."

"A'ight. What time are you headin' over there?"

"In an hour or so."

"A'ight. I'll meet you there."

"Bet."

Once the call ended, I hopped to my feet with a huge grin on my face; a young hood nigga was eager to get dressed and head out before the firework show started.

"Them fuck niggas ain't gon' know what hit they asses by the time them motherfuckin' bullets slam into their bodies," I voiced before laughing.

***

The sun shined brightly as the wind blessed our hot bodies with a little bit of cool air. A mixture of songs from TK Soul loudly played from Ms. Suelle's radio speakers, and t. The aroma of great tasting food permeated the air. My stomach growled as differently shaped kids ran about doing what kids did. With cups in their hands, people bobbed their heads, danced, and enjoyed the company of others.

I sauntered towards Ms. Suelle's front door with Trandall behind me. I had to show some love to the host. Upon seeing her sitting on the porch with a group of ladies who were well-known gossipers, Trandall and I spoke and hugged them before we stepped inside the packed house.

As I quickly scanned the heavily populated crib for Sasha and Myia, I became impatient as laughter and chit-chat popped off. Making our way towards our hangout spot, I was stopped by one of Sasha's cousins who had her eyes on me. I brushed the chick off.

"That's why Sasha ain't stun' yo' ass anyway. She's here wit' *another* nigga anyways … he feedin' her an' shit," the hurt broad spat.

Trandall pushed me towards a closed door, leading to a room we used to hangout in when the crowd was too much for us. Turning the door knob, my anger showed the moment I saw Myia and Big Juke all boo'd up watching T.V. while Sasha had her tongue so far down Big Nuke's throat she could've choked the nigga.

"Sasha," Myia called out oddly.

"So, you can really sit up in this bitch an' tongue kiss this nigga, parade this nigga 'round like he ain't just popped yo' ass in the back of yo' head som' weeks back? You gon' act like--," I nastily stated before Myia stood and told me to calm down.

"I know damn well you ain't talkin' to me, Myia!" I shot back as I waltzed further into the room as they looked at me.

Trandall grabbed my left wrist, trying to pull me back, but I wasn't having that shit. I snatched my shit back and snarled at him with an ugly facial expression.

"Don't get pussy now, Trandall!" I shouted at my cousin who had been pissing me off lately.

"Marlon, why are you carrying on like this for? It's not like I led you on. Ever since Lil' Boo died, I was very clear about us. We are not going to be like that anymore," Sasha said as she didn't remove her body from Big Nuke's.

The look on his face made me want to do something to him myself; however, I had a child that I had to stay out of prison for. I couldn't wait until those niggas from the club wipe that smug look off his face and replace it with a still facial expression.

"You are in my grandmother's home carrying on like you don't have any fucking sense. The last thing you want to do is piss me off. Once I'm pissed off, everyone in this motherfucker will feel my wrath. I am no longer holding my emotions, Marlon. The best thing you can fucking do is move the fuck around. I'm done taking your shit and anyone else's for that matter!" she yelled as she glared at me while rubbing her bushy hair.

"You're just somethin' fo' him to do at the moment, guh. Why can't you see that?" I questioned as I pointed at Big Nuke.

Chuckling, he stood, but Sasha told him to sit back down. He did while growling.

"Yeah, do what yo' *commander* said, lil' puppet ass nigga," I nastily voiced as I held my eyes on him.

"Marlon, take it easy mane. Righteously, we can get som' food an' leave. That's what we came here to do anyways," Trandall voiced, sternly.

"You on these niggas side nih?" I asked as I placed my eyes on my six foot one, medium-brown skinned cousin.

"I'm on the side of *not* bein' disrespectful in Ms. Suelle's home."

Laughing, I replied, "Oh really? Last time I checked, som' years back, you got yo' dick sucked in Ms. Suelle's bedroom … on her bed to be exact."

"Marlon, that's enough!" Myia spat as she stood, walking towards me.

When she stood up so did Big Juke. He stared at me as if he wanted to kill me. Chuckling at him, I nodded my head.

"You need to go right now!" Myia screamed while pushing me towards the door.

"Get yo' fuckin' hands off me. I'on know where they been."

"Nigga, you better watch yo' fuckin' mouth when talkin' to my girl!" Big Juke said as he began to stroll towards me.

Big Nuke hopped to his feet and grabbed his cousin all the while telling him in a tone that I didn't like, "Calm down. We gon' give this nigga a pass. After all, he's feelin' salty 'bout the women that's been in his life since he's been on this earth. He's also salty that he was caught up in the trance wit' a tranny. Not to mention, that he's got som' personal issues goin' on wit' his kid."

Before I knew it, I was trying my best to get to Big Nuke. I was beyond aggressive with getting Myia out of my way; so aggressive that I shoved her extremely hard to the ground. Trandall tried to pull me towards the door, but I didn't give up without a fight. Trandall and I ended up tussling, resulting in me getting the best of him. Once he was on the ground, the powerful cousins looked at me with a blank yet stern facial expression.

"I want it to be known that I don't give two fucks 'bout y'all. The day y'all die is the day I will celebrate heavily!" I told them as I was inches away from them.

The moment they took a step forward, Sasha sternly and nastily yelled, "Sit the fuck down, Big Juke and Zy'Lon. Don't make another fucking move, and I mean it. Marlon, if you don't leave my grandmother's home this fucking instant … you will fucking regret coming through that damn door because I will watch them whoop your ass something awful."

"So, Sasha, you finna be a common whore fo' Big Nuke, huh?" I angrily questioned as I looked at her.

"Fuck this shit," Big Nuke growled before gunning for me.

Myia yelled for Sasha and Big Juke to stop things, but neither of them said a word as the fight between Big Nuke and I took place. I was glad that there was minimal furniture in the hangout spot. My body was slammed on the ground and up against the wall so many times that I knew if furniture was in the large-sized room, it would've been broken.

The fight lasted until Ms. Suelle sauntered into the room and yelled, "Sasha, what in the hell is going on?"

"Marlon, got out of hand. He was way too disrespectful for no reason, Grandma."

Standing up as I wiped the blood from my mouth and nose, I spat, "I'm disrespectful? Really, Sasha?"

The glare she gave me could've murdered me if looks could kill.

"Marlon, you need to leave, honey. I'll fix you a plate," Ms. Suelle said softly as she looked at me.

Pissed off that she wanted me to leave instead of Big Juke and Big Nuke, I respectfully said, "Those two niggas should be the ones that leave. They are no good fo' Myia an' Sasha. They kidnapped all fo' of us som' weeks ago. Big Nuke knocked Sasha out before placin' her in the back of a van, which my child, Quinn, an' Trandall were already in. Those niggas are goin' to corrupt them. They made Sasha a commander of som' illegal stuff, and they're goin' to have her in a lot of trouble on top of doin' her dirty like they do *all* the females they deal wit'."

Before Ms. Suelle could utter a word, Sasha was standing with her hands on her thin hips as she evilly glared into my face. The look she gave me sent chills through my body.

Cocking her head to the right as she held the same facial expression, the woman I was willing to fly straight for said, "If you don't get the hell off this property, I will show you just how corrupt I can be. This is your final warning, Marlon."

As she walked off, Big Nuke, Big Juke, Myia, and Trandall were on her heels. Ms. Suelle looked at me with a disappointed facial expression. I could barely look into her pretty, brown eyes.

"Marlon, you have no right to come into my home and pick a fight of any kind. You were not raised this way, and I know this for a fact. Whatever happened between you and my granddaughter is over. Accept it and move on, son. I didn't say a word when you beat her and humiliated her to the point that she wanted to die ... hell, she was close to dying if her mother hadn't come into her home. You need to leave my house right now."

By the time Sasha approached the door, she coldly voiced, "Not beat me out of this house and see what's going to happen. You want to half ass expose some stuff, then I will full throttle expose some shit."

Turning around, I exited the hangout room. Folks were asking what happened, but none of us said a damn word. As I left, my phone dinged. Retrieving it out of my pocket, I looked at the note that I put in their Friday night after I left the club. With a smile on my face, I skipped out of the door that the others didn't go through. Pulling out a blunt, I fired it up.

"Aye, let me hit that, Marlon," an unknown individual said from the left of me.

"Nawl, ain't no sharin' this way," I replied as I didn't turn around to look the nigga in his face.

Niggas killed me with that bumming a cigarette and blunt shit. If you didn't have money for the habit, then don't ask the next for theirs. I only shared with a few people. As I tugged on my blunt, I zipped off into my own world.

Ring. Ring. Ring.

Not looking at the screen on my phone, I answered the call—still in my own world.

"Hello?"

"Hey, what time are you coming up to the hospital?" my mother inquired.

"I'll be leaving out in twenty minutes. You need anything?"

"Yes. Some food from Ms. Suelle's house."

"Okay. I'll bring y'all a little bit of everyth--," I stated before I was cut off by the sound of rapid gunfire blasting in close range.

As my body and my phone dropped, people screamed, ran, and dropped to the ground. I didn't close my eyes because I wanted to see those fuck niggas die. I was going to rejoice in the name of Jesus for those niggas not being on this earth anymore.

It seemed as if the gunfire was never going to stop as a white old school van with tinted windows zoomed down the road still shooting. The skirting of tires was the reason I hopped to my feet, but a gut-wrenching scream from Sasha's mouth and other women were the reasons I ran towards their voices. As I ran, I prayed that Trandall and Myia weren't hurt. I prayed that my ill intentions didn't fall on those I dearly cared about.

"Somebody call 911!" several people shouted from every direction.

"Not my babies! Not my babies!" a woman wailed from the side porch.

What in the fuck have I done?

"Who in the fuck was those niggas after?" a strong, deep, male voice asked as my stomach turned inside out at the sound of the woman crying about her kids. From the tone of her wails, her kids were dead.

"Momma! Momma! Where is my momma?" Sasha's mother screamed loudly before she started crying.

I only wanted Big Juke an' Big Nuke dead ... not no fuckin' kids.

"Trandall! Sasha! Myia!" I yelled out as I rounded the corner of the house.

"Oh, god, not my--," Sasha's mother said before a group of people yelled out commands to catch her.

Where in the fuck are they? I thought as I stopped dead in my tracks on the side of the house closest to the front door.

My heart fell to my feet as my peepers landed upon a scene that I never thought I would see in my fucking life—Ms. Suelle dead with half her face blown off as Sasha rocked her back and forth while Big Nuke tightly held on to Sasha. Big Juke tied a piece of cloth around Myia's right thigh, and Trandall was lying on his back holding his side.

As I dropped to the ground with blurred vision, I looked at my cousin as he glared at me with eyes that said he knew what I had done.

I'm sorry. I'm so fuckin' sorry.

"Whoever did this … I want them in my fucking face immediately," Sasha spoke without an ounce of emotion as she glared at her deceased grandmother.

Chapter 17

Sasha

Wednesday, June 30th

It had been three days since the shooting at my grandmother's house, and I was still like a zombie. As I was balled in the corner of my sofa watching the rain beat down on my balcony as thunder and lightning showed face, my mind was on my grandmother and the two small children who died that day. I couldn't get the image out of my head of the people who were traumatized—screaming, yelling, and had blood all over them.

I was determined to find the people behind the shooting. I wasn't going to rest until they felt what the fuck my family and I felt. I wasn't going to be satisfied until my pain ran into their lives, causing them to see pain at its finest. I was bent on not being a devil; however, at a time like this, I had no fucking choice but to become one.

I couldn't handle the task of being a part of the funeral arrangements my mother and Momma Linda wanted me to be a part of. I wasn't ready to say goodbye to my grandma; I wasn't ready to pick out a casket. I needed her in my life. She was my true rock even though I acted like she wasn't. I guess that's what hurt me the most. I wasn't there for her like I had been before Zy'Lon came along.

As I rehashed the past, I tried my best to see how the shootout took place in the calm city of Prattville. Who in the hell were the people after and why? I tried my best to place the slow creeping white van that everyone saw but didn't pay it any mind until it was too late.

I called a meeting the moment the coroner placed my grandmother and the children's bodies in a bag. I didn't see Myia or Trandall safely to the hospital; instead, I sent Big Juke in my place. Zy'Lon took me to my apartment so that I could shower and get dressed. While I showered, I had a speech ready for those under my wing. I had specific orders for them, but once I got in their presence, that prepared speech went out the window as my nasty emotions took over. I ordered them to bring me the fuckers who had a hand in the shit. I wanted them to feel my wrath before I shot them the same way they did my grandmother and those poor children who were just playing.

During the meeting, I met the big wigs of the assassin organization. Instantly, they liked me. The way I looked, dressed, carried myself, and reeked of power and ruthless intentions, they didn't want me to step down. But, when I told them that no assassination attempts would take place without proper evidence as to why, they began to murmur and say shit under their breaths. Not in the mood for bullshit, I looked at Big Juke, and he placed two bullets in the heads of two men who had a lot to say without mumbling. At that precise moment, everyone in the fucking room knew that I meant business.

By Zy'Lon's body language and stern facial expression, I knew that he wasn't pleased with my choice of having those two men killed, but I didn't give a fuck; I was in a killing mood. Their comments and the thought of my grandmother dead in my arms turned me into a being that I was sure no one wanted to see. I made damn sure of that!

After we left the brief meeting, we went by the hospital. Myia had to have extensive surgery, which she was still in. Three bullets ripped through her ligaments and muscles, leaving her leg messed up to the point that she needed a rod in it. She was forever going to walk with a horrible limp.

Trandall was shot on his side. He was still in surgery when I arrived as well. His large and small intestines were damaged, so there was a high possibility that they were going to put a colostomy bag on him. Whether they were going to do a reversal surgery or not, we didn't know.

"You've been to yo' self long enough. Come here, Sasha," Zy'Lon softly voiced, interrupting my thinking process.

Nodding my head, I crawled into his lap and laid my head down. I sighed heavily as I closed my eyes.

"Juke called an' said that Myia an' Trandall are doin' okay. They're in pain, but both are walkin' 'round. They'll be released from the hospital within two or three days," he spoke softly as he massaged the backs of my hands.

"Okay."

"Sasha, we need to talk."

"I already know what you're going to say ... you don't approve of how I handled those guys at the meeting," I rattled off as I opened my eyes and placed them on his handsome face.

"No, that's not what I was 'bout to say. You did what you had to do to make them see that it was yo' way or the highway 'til you leave the throne to someone else," he spoke quickly before continuing, "Juke learned who the individual was that orchestrated the shootin', why it took place, an' who carried the shit out."

Sitting upright, I glared into his face as I patiently waited for him to drop the names and their locations.

"Marlon," was all he said.

Shaking my head, I said, "Can't be."

"It was, an' I know that you're a factual person. Juke made sure to get the evidence that supports what the shooters an'and other witnesses had to say 'bout Marlon bein' in the shooters' presence. Those same shooters are niggas that don't like Big Juke an' me. They be tryin' to set us up fo' the longest, an' each time they fail."

"I want to see everything and everyone … now," I said as I lifted off the sofa.

"Sasha, I need you to grant me to be commander over this situation. Shit is too personal, an' youll go 'bout it the wrong way."

"No. I'm going to get dressed ... I suggest you do the same."

"I told Juke not to pick up Marlon. I was sure that you wanted to deal wit' him yo' self," he told me as he was on my heels, turning me around to face him.

As I gazed into his handsome eyes, I gently stroked his beard all the while thinking of how much I adored him. Since the death of my grandmother, the look in Zy'Lon's eyes was different. I saw sadness, hope, and something else that I couldn't quite put a name on it. I wanted to speak with him about it, but I didn't know where to begin.

"Thank you," I told him as I felt the need to have him close to me.

Biting his bottom lip in a way that showed his golds, I sexily growled.

"Fuck me," I moaned as I placed my hand inside of his gym shorts.

There was nothing else for him to say. Scooping me into his arms, Zy'Lon carried me to my bed and put it all the fucking way down. As I wanted him to fuck me, he didn't; he made love to me in such a passionate, caring way that had tears sliding down my face. While I cried and came, Zy'Lon whispered sweet things in my ear before giving me an offer that I had to ponder.

By the climax of our wonderful passion, I joyfully screamed, "Yess, Zy'Lon. Yess!"

Two hours later, we were in a rundown-looking house in Tuscaloosa—the same house Zy'Lon had to come to pick up the snitch bitch that I caught sucking on Marlon's dick. As we stepped through the raggedy place, my head was held high as my eyes were low and filled with hatred while I glared into the eyes of those who carried out a horrendous act.

"I only need one person to talk," I voiced loudly and without any emotions.

On demand, one motherfucker talked, and I actively listened. I paced back and forth as I received the news about what happened, why, and who actually carried out the plan. There were eight niggas involved in the shit, including Marlon. The female who saw Marlon talking to the niggas was also present. She told me what she saw and thought she heard when Marlon stepped from the back of the club. Intrigued by it all, the chick who saw Marlon talking to the shooters was the same broad that left the club with him; her name was Dejah.

"Get everybody's phone numbers," I ordered.

Big Juke and Zy'Lon did as I asked, but Big Juke had a confused look on his face.

Thus, I placed a smile on mine before saying, "I'll inform you shortly."

"The only person who is free to go is Dejah," I told Zy'Lon.

"A'ight."

Before the chick left, I asked her, "If Marlon hadn't kicked you to the curb, would you be in my presence right now?"

"How did you know he kicked me to the curb?" she asked curiously in a low tone.

Chuckling, I replied, "No offense, but you aren't his type."

"Wow ... um, no, I wouldn't be here if he hadn't kicked me to the curb," she said with a curt attitude.

"I would adjust that attitude accordingly. I didn't fuck you and toss you out of my home. You have a blessed day, sweetie," I replied as I waved her ass out of my face.

I didn't want to be nasty with the chick; I just wanted to keep it real with her. If Marlon had treated her like gold, she wouldn't have said a bitch ass thing about what she saw or *thought* she heard. I felt bad for the broad. It seemed as if she was a good chick, just looking for love. She sort of reminded me of myself.

"What do you want me to do wit' them?" Big Juke asked with a raised eyebrow.

"Zy'Lon will tell you exactly what I want done," I announced as I looked at each of those raggedy-looking-ass niggas.

Ring. Ring. Ring.

"Hello?" I said as I walked out of the rundown house.

"Hey, sweetheart, how are you?" Momma Linda inquired softly.

"I'm okay," I sighed as I placed my eyes on the poverty-stricken neighborhood I was in.

"Okay. I was just calling to check on you."

"K. Thank you, Momma Linda. How are you? Marlia? Grandma Sylvia? Marlon?" I asked while strolling towards Zy'Lon's truck.

"Marlia is doing good. They're moving her to a different room by the end of the week. Momma is heartbroken. Marlon is sick. I told him to stay home and that I would care for Marlia while he got himself together. My poor son is having it rough. Hell, we all are. Me ... I have to be strong for y'all, so I'm okay."

Your poor son is having shit rough because he's the one who orchestrated this shit. All because he couldn't have me.

Continuing, she said, "Will you go by there and check on him for me? I know he would be pleased to see you."

Once she learned who was behind this shit, she was surely going to be heartbroken. When the strong Quad that she had the pleasure of raising fell apart, she's going to feel like she failed; that was surely going to bring disappointment and further heart break her way.

With an ugly facial expression on my face, I replied, "Yes, ma'am. Will you kiss Grandma Sylvia and Marlia for me please?"

"Absolutely," she breathed into the phone, "Did your mom inform you of the funeral arrangements for Ms. Suelle?"

That question was too much for me as my stomach rumbled and tumbled. The next thing you know I was hunched over, spilling contents from my breakfast and lunch.

"Are you okay, Sasha?" Momma Linda and Zy'Lon asked in unison.

As I continued to vomit, I nodded my head. When Zy'Lon approached me, he rubbed my back. My body welcomed his soothing touch.

"I'll call and check on you later on today, okay?" Momma Linda voiced softly before telling me that she loved me.

"Okay and I love you more," I said weakly as Zy'Lon handed me his shirt.

With the call ended and my stomach somewhat returning to normal, I stood erect as wiped my mouth with his white shirt.

"I see now that we gotta keep napkins an' shit on us, huh?" he joked with a weak smile on his face.

"Yes."

"The other person on the line mentioned the wrong word, huh?" he probed as a bunch of birds started cawing.

I nodded my head as I exhaled sharply. The word funeral had never been an issue for me until the day I held my grandmother's corpse. Every time someone called my phone mentioning her homegoing celebration, I was running to the kitchen's trashcan or the bathroom.

At one point in time, Zy'Lon asked me several times if I was pregnant, and, of course, I told him no but the truth was I didn't know. It wasn't like Zy'Lon and I used protection. I didn't ask him to pull out, and he sure as hell didn't. However, I was certain that I wasn't pregnant because I had a period at the end of April which ran into the beginning days of the May.

"Is it time to go?"

"Yep. To Marlon's crib," I said as I waltzed towards the passenger side.

"What do you have planned fo' him? Sasha, you can't handle this situation like you did the big wigs. You gotta have a better plan other than killin' him."

"I want his ass dead, just like my grandmother and those precious children. He has to go ... point blank period," I spoke clearly as I sat in the passenger seat.

After Zy'Lon nodded his head, he placed a kiss on my forehead while gently rubbing my stomach. With a raised eyebrow, I looked at him with a curious facial expression.

"What? A nigga can't rub yo' stomach now? A nigga can't wishful think?"

"Wishful think for what, Zy'Lon?" I asked sexily with a weak smile on my face.

Blushing, he said, "We got business to handle. So can we focus on that?"

"Sure."

After he closed the door, my cellphone rang. Looking at the screen on my phone, I saw Myia's name. Quickly, I answered.

"Hello?"

"Hey, how are you?" she asked before sighing.

"As good as I can be. How are you?" I questioned as Zy'Lon hopped in his truck and started the engine.

"In pain, waiting on these damn nurses to come in. Are you coming by today?"

"Yes. Is there anything that you need?"

"Food ... *real* damn food," she said weakly before laughing.

"What exactly do you want?"

"Whatever you bring is fine."

"Okay. I'll surprise you with a meal that will put your ass to sleep," I joked.

"Good, I need that in my life. Those images are etched into my brain, Sasha. The way that Ms. S--," she stated before I cut her off.

"Alright, Myia, that's enough. I'm having issues right now. My stomach is weak as fuck at the mention of certain things, so can we please not discuss anything of that nature?" I begged in a tone she was used to hearing me talk in.

"Okay. Um … um," she continued to say repeatedly.

"It's okay, Myia, just no talks of that right now," I informed her as my stomach became unsettled again.

"Okay. Did you talk to Trandall?"

"No. Why?"

"He said some things that got me worried and scared for my brother. I hope it was just the medicine that caused him to say those things, but Sasha I fear what Trandall said was true."

"Rest up. I'll be there before you know it. Okay?"

"Okay."

"I love you, Myia."

"I love you more."

After the call ended, I looked at Zy'Lon and said, "I need you to go to Baptist South before we go to Marlon's crib."

"How do you know he's home?"

"Trust, I know his ass is there. Momma Linda, his mother, made sure to tell me to go by there and check on him."

"Sasha, baby, I don't thi--," Zy'Lon stated before I cut him off.

"Shit, has to happen this way. I won't have it any other way."

 Chapter 18

Marlon

I had been shook ever since the day I left Ms. Suelle's yard with three murders on my hands, two injured family members, and a well-loved individual who couldn't cry at the sight of her grandmother dead in her arms with half of her face blown off. I've been haunted by Ms. Suelle and the young children during the night when I tried to sleep. In order to cease the nightmares that plagued me something awful, I drank myself until I passed out. I couldn't look myself in the mirror. I barely visited or called my sister or Trandall. I was all types of fucked up.

To my surprise, I received a call from Sasha saying that she would be at my crib within forty minutes. The look on my face was priceless as I didn't know how to feel about her coming over. I didn't know if she wanted to be by my side because of what had went down and how she was feeling, or because she realized that I was the one she really needed in her life. Whatever the case was, I quickly got myself together as I cleaned the little mess I had in the kitchen.

After I cared for my body and home, I sank into a low spot as my mental wouldn't let me forget about the shit I had done. Taking a seat on the sofa, I cried harder than I did when I first arrived home after I witnessed the coroner placing three black body bags in the back of the van. I balled my eyes out as images of those children happily playing before the white van crept down the road. They were giggling and running about with smiles on their faces and Popsicle stains on their light-colored shirts.

Unlike the woman who lost her children, I would be able to see, hold, and discipline Marlia. The thought of my daughter and the children-less mother caused me to hate myself even more than what I did when I saw Ms. Suelle's hardly recognizable face.

"I don't deserve to be a father after what I've done. I don't deserve to give my baby happiness when a mother is suffering as she has to live her life without her kids," I sobbed into my hands as the doorbell chimed.

Knowing who was at the door, I looked at it several moments before getting myself together.

Wiping my face and clearing my throat several times, I hopped to my feet and said, "Coming."

Rapidly, I unlocked the door. As I opened it, I wasn't expecting Sasha to have Big Nuke with her. The facial expression she gave me placed me in a horrible spirit.

"Why is he at my home wit' you?" I inquired calmly.

She didn't respond with words; instead, she responded by rushing me towards my door with her hands around my neck and a gun to my stomach. Glaring into my face, she growled, and her nostrils flared. I knew she wanted to cry.

Lord, please, don't let her know what I've done.

"What's wrong?" I asked as she tightened her grip around my neck.

"Please, tell me that you didn't orchestrate that shooting so that Big Juke and Zy'Lon would be killed. Please tell me that ain't so, Marlon."

I wanted to lie, but I couldn't. I wanted to look away, but I couldn't. I wanted to close my eyes, but I wouldn't dare close them for fear of seeing the images that I drank myself unconscious to run away from.

Big Nuke closed the door while shaking his head. After locking it, he walked towards the couch while whistling. I didn't have an ill thought about the nigga; my focus was on the one person who I *never* wanted to hurt—Sasha.

"How could you do something so fucking careless like that? For what? Because I didn't want you in my life like that anymore?" she asked as her voice broke and a tear slid down her beautiful chocolate face.

I didn't say anything because I didn't have the correct response.

"Are you going to fucking say something, Marlon?"

"I don't know what I can say to make things right, Sasha. There's nothin' fo' me to say."

Huffing, she removed her hands away from my neck before backing up. With her moist, hurt-filled eyes planted on me, she shook her head. An eerie silence overtook my home, and I couldn't shake the feeling that some shit was about to go down. Placing my eyes on Big Nuke, he had a facial expression plastered across his face that concerned me.

Sasha growled—the type of growl that made my soul weak and spirit sad. I wasn't afraid that she was going to kill me. I was afraid of her making me suffer, which would forever put her in a dark place. I didn't want Sasha to turn into a revengeful, hateful person. I didn't want her past and current hurts to torture her at night. I didn't want anything that I nor anyone else did to her stop her from being the beautiful person she was. My actions were not going to be the reason that Sasha resulted to killing in order to soothe the pain she felt.

"Rita Langsford lost her two children because you had your ass on your shoulders! Rita is mourning the only children she would ever have! Rita almost lost her life giving birth to those kids, Marlon, the same kids that you help murder because you couldn't accept the fact that I chose someone who's good for me. You're a fucking father; how could you do some shit like that? You were fucking mad because I didn't want you for the simple fact that you put your hands on me, and blamed me for the loss of a friend that you killed in a got damn car accident. You took the one person away from me who had my back through rain, sleet, hail, and snow. Not only did you fuck up my life and Rita's ... you forever fucked up your sister's and Trandall's. The same ones you failed to visit and care for. Myia has a rod in her fucking leg. It will *never* come out. She will walk with a mean limp, and Trandall's intestines were damaged badly to the point that he has to wear a fucking shit bag for the rest of his got damn life. I learned that tonight by talking to one of his nurses. Imagine how he feels. You gone pay for how we feel. Oh bitch ass nigga, you're gonna fucking feel me," Sasha snarled as she cocked the gun back and aimed it at me.

Her eyes were a pretty shade of brown, but, at that moment, they seemed black and void of love and joy. Taking a deep breath, I had to make things right. I didn't need her being in hell with me.

"Sasha, I'll make you a deal," I said as I saw the gun shaking in her hand.

"No, fuck boy, you don't get to make a deal with me," she said loudly as Big Nuke strolled towards her.

"No, baby, this isn't the way. You will never come back from this if you go through wit' it. I told you this situation is different than the others. You're different. I don't want this lifestyle fo' you. Use another alternative, Sasha. You've done enough," Big

Nuke voiced softly as he took the gun away from Sasha and tucked it into the back of his jeans.

"I'll forever hate you, Marlon Boyd. As of today, you are really no longer in my life. You don't exist to me, and I mean that."

"I'll take you hatin' me versus you goin' to the dark side forever," I told her as she glared at me.

"Stay the fuck away from me. Don't try to communicate with me or none of that shit. If I so much as get wind that you're trying to come after Zy'Lon and Big Juke, I won't hesitate to kill you. There's no telling who you will have murdered as your useless ass shooters can't aim."

For God knows how long, we stared at each other.

Clearing her throat, Sasha said, "You're a waste of breath, Marlon. I hate to say this shit, but, oh-motherfucking-well, you should've been rinsed down the sink. Fuck swallowing ... you ain't even good enough to sit in the pit of Momma Linda's stomach."

From the time I watched them walk out of my crib, Sasha's words stuck to me so bad that I knew I wasn't shit. Dropping to my knees, I threw my head back as I closed my eyes. I knew what I had to do;

thus, I prayed to God that He help my family and daughter would have strength, courage, and love for me. I prayed that they didn't turn their backs on me as I turned my back against everything they taught me.

I've made a mess of my life. There's only one way to fix this shit. God, please, forgive me for my sins.

Chapter 19

Zy'Lon

Thursday, August 23rd

The past two months had been interesting and less challenging. I thought Juke and I were going to catch hell from exiting the assassin world, but, unbeknownst to us, we had no issues getting out. The remaining bigwigs let us go without any threats or harsh words.

Juke's ass had to ask why they let us go so freely, and their response was, "That beautiful woman has been hurt, and she's the type of female that we don't want sitting on an assassin's throne. Plus, she made it clear that we had to let you guys go freely without any problems, or our worlds would be shaken beyond belief. Let's just say that she's smarter than she looks. Damn woman had pictures of our mistresses, wives, and other little toys, so you know her threats were heard loud and clear. Quite frankly, you guys can tell her that the request for Johnnie to take over has been granted. She's no longer commander."

That shit was music to my ears. I didn't want either of us to be looking over our shoulders for the rest of our lives. We didn't want the women in our lives afraid for us to leave the house, on pins and needles whenever the phone rang; that wasn't a way for them to live. Hell, I wouldn't want to live like that.

Juke became accustomed to being there for Myia. After Myia was released from the hospital, he demanded that he move in with her until she was able to move around by herself. Of course, she didn't protest. She wanted to be around him more now than ever. I loved seeing them together. They were perfect for each other. He was hard core, and she mellowed out his yellow ass. He stopped referring to her as his "damsel in distress". Now, she was referred to as "baby". I never saw him so happy. Juke finally found love—let me rephrase that, that nigga finally let someone love him other than his parents and me. They were expecting a baby in the upcoming year; she was new new type of pregnant.

The night after we left Marlon's crib, he turned himself and the shooters in. They were currently at Autauga County Metro Jail without bond.

Last month, Sasha finally cried her eyes out about the loss of her grandmother. I was glad she finally let those demons go. I was even happier seeing her resume to the person I had come to love via talks with Charles.

Seeing that Sasha had forgiven her parents, I knew that I had to do the same. Two weeks ago, I made a trip to one of the dope houses that I used to serve out of. Upon seeing my strung-out mother begging one of the guys that I promoted to my position, I gave him a crisp, ome-hundred dollar bill to give her a nice hit. Crazy, right? Yep, but, oh well I was in her presence for the last time to inform her that I forgave her. Of course, she didn't understand the severity of shit. All she wanted was her next high. After I said what I had to say, I left, aiming for the other place that I used to trap at. Once I laid eyes on the nigga who aided my mother in making me, I paid another runner one-hundred dollars before I told my father that I forgave him too.

"Son, I didn't mean for this shit to overtake us. Never in a million years would I have thought that I would be using the very product that I used to sell. I never thought that we would be so weak for this drug. I'm sorry that we put you through so much hell, Zy'Lon. You need to get out of this game and do better than your mother and me," he stated as his eyes rolled in the back of his head as his body trembled.

Nodding my head, I made my peace and left. Sasha was waiting for me with a concerned expression on her face. She asked me how I felt, and I told her that I was fine—thanks to her wanting to be in my life.

"I just didn't want to be in your life, Zy'Lon. I *need* to be in your life," she said as she brought her head close to mine, initiating a kiss that had me ready to dive off in her.

From that day forward, we made our relationship official. I wasn't just her protector; I was her young hood nigga, and I wore that title with pride. Every time a bitch approached me, I was quick to tell them that I was taken. When niggas tried to step to Sasha, she cut them off quick with a sexy reply of, "*I got a young hood nigga who will lay it down about me, so your best bet is to get out my face.*"

I loved when she let me know she was all into me and me only. That just made the love making even better.

"So, when are we goin' to that damn crib you inherited in Dubai?" Juke asked the moment Sasha and Myia strolled into the hangout spot of my crib in Tuscaloosa.

"Funny, Myia and I were just talking about that, Jy'Lon," she said as they took a seat on the long, comfortable, gray suede sofa.

Once we left the streets, so did our nicknames. Jy'Lon finally took a liking to being called by his government name, not that he had a choice anyways. Myia made sure of that.

Continuing, Sasha said, "I was thinking about us going soon. I have some last minute things I need to take care of concerning the rental properties in Orlando and the Midwest."

"A'ight, let us know so we can start preparing for the trip," Juke replied as the ladies cellphones dinged.

Sasha hopped to her feet running as Myia took her time getting up. Juke assisted her, and she softly and genuinely told him thank you like she always did.

Once Myia was out of earshot, I asked, "How's she really doin'?"

"Today is a bad day fo' her. She misses her brother, an' her leg hurts like hell. There isn't too much medicine she can take because of the pregnancy an' all."

"I hope things get better fo' her real soon."

"Me too, man, me too," he voiced as the women reappeared.

As Sasha helped Myia take a seat, Juke and I looked at them. They had some shit up their sleeves, and I pondered who was going to leak the press. Straddling me, Sasha gently tugged on my goatee as she gazed into my eyes lovingly.

"What's up, Sexy Chocolate?" I asked as I snuggled further into the sofa with my hands on the small of my lady's back.

"What do you think of this ... Zy'Lon Junior or a Zy'Lona?" she asked with a huge smile on her face.

"Null nih!" Juke and I loudly spat in unison.

Smiling from ear-to-ear, she said, "We're pregnant, Zy'Lon."

As I placed my hand on her belly, I brought her face close to mine and sucked on her bottom lip before attacking her fruity tasting tongue. When she groaned, I knew what time it was time for bedroom action.

"Um, Myia," I heard Juke say.

"Yes, honey?" she cooed lovingly.

"I'm hungry. Can you feed me?"

Instantly, I broke the kiss off and jokingly asked, "So, yo' mouth ain't a virgin no mo'?"

"His mouth been long gone from that virgin status," Myia replied, laughing.

"Well, hot damn," Sasha laughed before pointing towards the door.

***

Juke, Vincent, and I decided to cook dinner at my crib. Sasha invited her mother to formally meet us. Myia called her mom to come up with Sasha's mom, but she didn't want to come. According to Myia, her mother was down about Marlon, and she wasn't feeling social-able.

Everyone had a good time and enjoyed the exquisite meal that we cooked. Sasha's mother learned that Myia and Sasha were pregnant. Oh, the look in her eyes was spectacular. She gave them encouraging, beautiful words. -

Afterwards, she and Vincent hit it off. It was cool seeing him smiling and actually enjoying a conversation with a woman other than Juke's whack ass mother. Around ten o'clock, Vincent and Sasha's mother left together. According to them, they wanted to get out and have a little fun. Of course, I joked on Sasha and Juke. Once the jokes stopped, the freaky talk took place between Myia and Juke, and they were off to one of my guest rooms.

Lately, we had been staying together. The ladies wanted to be close to each other, and nothing changed about Juke and I being close. I had grown accustomed to the four of us being together. Myia and Sasha made us complete, and not a second went by that I regretted or wanted the new Quad to not be together as a whole.

"What are you thinking about, daddy-to-be?" Sasha sexily inquired as she sashayed into the living room, wearing a short, silk, chrome-hued robe.

"Just how good things are goin' wit' the fo' of us under one roof. How I'm goin' to love havin' you in my life day-in an' day-out," I told her as she straddled me.

"Funny, I was just lying across the bed thinking the same thing."

As she bit on her bottom lip, I placed her on her back. Seductively, Sasha spread her legs all the while looking at me as if I was a meal. I knew what she wanted, but I wasn't going to give it to her—not at the moment. Placing my hands on her soft, average-sized feet, I began massaging them. My eyes never left her brown peepers.

Kiss after kiss was strategically placed on the bottoms and tops of her feet as I massaged her ankles. The cutest coo left her mouth, causing me to chuckle. She reached out to me, grabbing a small section of my shoulder and pushing it towards her, indicating for me to come closer. I shook my head and mouthed no.

I took pleasure in seeing her squirm. I wanted my baby to know that her body was a temple, and that I would never rush pleasing every corner of it. While I blew on her thighs and massaged her legs, Sasha's back arched, a clear indication that she was beyond aroused and on the verge of exploding. As I mischievously glared into her face, I inhaled the sweet-scent coming from her lovely, fat, and hairless pussy.

My mouth watered for a taste of my lady. There was nothing like getting full off a woman that you're crazy about, nothing like going overboard for the one woman that you prayed would love you for you. Nothing was better than hearing Sasha moan, yell, coo, and whine my name or say that she loved how I treated her *in* and *out* of the bedroom. I prided myself on satisfying every inch of her. Whatever her desires were, I catered to them.

Before I slowly rose to her face, I planted six, long, tongue kisses on her pussy as I grabbed a handful of her booty.

"My god!" she groaned loudly as I had to keep her from throwing that good twat more on my lips.

Holding on tightly to her quivering body, I dragged my long, pink, flesh upwards, leaving tingling sensations from her pussy to her neck. Diving my tongue into her warm, minty mouth, Sasha groaned as she further opened her legs for me.

"I need you, Zy'Lon," she said after breaking our kiss as she glared into my eyes, lovingly.

"You got me. I ain't goin' nowhere, Sasha."

"Promise?" she asked in a child-like voice.

"Pinky promise at that," I sincerely replied before engaging in another heated kiss.

As Sasha was lost in a world of pure bliss, I thought it was time for us to go into her world for a minute, the world that I badly wanted to release her from; the same world that Charles wanted me to break out of her. Seeing that she enjoyed being there sexually, I took pleasure in growling in her ear before standing and sternly looking at her as if she did something wrong.

"You have five-point-eight-seconds to get yo' ass to Zy'Sa's Erotic Temple," I barked with a wicked smile on my face as I stroked my goatee.

The look in my woman's eyes as I called out our locked playroom was priceless. I had been waiting on the right time to summon her ass to the room Juke and I put together based off the things Sasha had told me about. The look on Juke's face when he learned what I had in store for the medium-sized room that sat across from our bedroom was comical. After he learned of the costs of the sexual items and furniture, that nigga's eyes were big as he coughed for ten minutes straight.

Juke knew what I had in mind since earlier today when we put the final touches on the playroom, so I didn't have to worry about him or Myia coming out of the room—well, for at least fifteen minutes. I had to warn him that if he came out of his room at a certain time, he was going to catch me doing some extremely grown folks' shit. Of course, he joked. Then, he asked me exactly what I was going to do. I never kept too many things from him, so I told him. The look on my face was priceless when he told me that he had already ate the booty like groceries courtesy of Myia

"Are you serious right now?" she asked with a huge smile on her face, bringing me into reality.

"Get yo' ass to Zy'Sa's Erotic Temple, Sexy Chocolate." I ordered with a stern facial expression.

As she hopped to her feet with a huge smile on her face, Sasha ran from the front room happy as fuck.

I laughed before saying, "Yo' ass better be careful wit' our precious cargo, or we ain't gon' play yo' way."

"Yes, sir," she cooed loudly.

Her voiced sounded muffled, so I knew she was in a submissive position.

Running my hand down my face, I mumbled, "Let's see how this goes."

We never acted out anything, but I did watch videos about the shit Sasha liked. There were plenty of things to learn, so I told her three days a week I wanted her to point me in the right direction.

As I ambled towards Zy'Sa's Erotic Temple, I had the perfect view of my woman as that beautiful arch was in her back, that juicy booty of hers was tooted high in the air, and her hands were placed at the right angle in front of the door as her head rested on her wrists. Amping things up my way, I walked behind Sasha and kneeled.

"What's the safe word, Sexy Chocolate?" I spoke in a dominant way.

"Our baby," she spoke in an aroused tone.

"Good, Sexy Chocolate," I replied as I inserted two fingers inside of her dripping wet, hot hole.

"You gon' behave tonight, Sexy Chocolate?" I asked voiced as I found that walnut-sized thing that would make her go crazy and leak profusely onto my fingers.

"Yes, sir," she whined as she began twerking on my fingers.

I popped her bottom before saying, "Nope. You stay still. No movin' until I say so."

She giggled and replied, "Yes, sir."

I noticed that Sasha had a thing for being spanked; thus, I catered to that as well. I made sure not to pop her too hard or too soft. I hit that ass with just the right amount of force that had her on the verge of cumm'ing and yelling.

"You do know that you gotta be quiet, right? That is until we get inside of the room," I told her in my regular tone.

"I know," she breathed erratically.

Carrying on with my tasks, I fingered fucked Sasha as I did something I never thought I would do—eat her ass. I couldn't lie as if I didn't like it. A nigga was even more amped for the rest of our night until the early morning. Once I finished devouring my woman as she was in the submissive position, I unlocked the door and commanded for her to walk in.

"Zy'Lon!" she excitedly screamed as she turned to face me as her eyes were moist.

"What I did nih?" I asked as if I didn't know what had her so amazed and happy.

"Oouu, we finna have some fun in this bitch tonight," she replied as she snatched me towards her.

"Fuck that just 'tonight' shit. We gonna have fun fo' the rest of our lives. I got you, Sexy Chocolate ... fo' eva," I told her as I took off her robe, exposing her beautiful body.

Lifting her up, I stepped across the threshold of the door. Once I closed and locked it, our wonderful, sensual night began. I left nothing untouched on Sasha's body as I placed her on different sex benches, seats, and towers. After our fourth round of loving, I told her that I wanted to spice things up a bit.

"What you mean? There's only so much that we can do with me being pregnant," she said, lying in my arms as we soaked in the tub.

"I want you to be my Domme," I whispered in her ear as my dick began to rise.

Turning around to face me, she had a sneaky smile on her face as her head was cocked to the right.

"My, oh, my, oh, my," she spoke sternly in that commander's tone that I loved so much.

Ah, shit, I thought as I bit down on my bottom lip, growling.

That power restored to her like it hadn't been weeks since she wore that hat. The flicker of love in her eyes never ceased from that moment until the early morning—when I took the power back of being the Dom.

"I'll always love, honor, respect, an' protect you an' our lil' one, Sasha. I'm gon' always be yo' number one rider. I love you, Sexy Chocolate," I told her as I carried her to our bedroom.

"I know," she said sleepily before placing a kiss on my neck.

My world was complete. I didn't need the streets or yearn for my parents' love and attention anymore. I had Sasha, Juke, Myia, and our babies. I was good. Shit, I was better than good; I was motherfucking great. There wasn't anything else that I needed. I had shit that was priceless—love for and from a woman who I would kill over.

A motherfucking young hood nigga fell in love; that's all I ever wanted.

Sasha

Wednesday, October 17th

What can I say other than I was happier than ever. I was rocking the baddest diamond ring that money could buy, thanks to Zy'Lon asking me to be his wife last month. I had the cutest little, rounded, pudge at the bottom of my stomach. He was more excited about my growing womb than I was. Every little move I tried to make, he was down my throat about moving too much. I had to tell him to chill. Who in the hell wanted to be sitting for hours upon hours as their man catered to them? Sure as hell not me. He would have his share of moving around a lot when I hit the third trimester, which wasn't any time soon.

Things between Zy'Lon and I had been great. He decided to sign up for college for the spring semester of the following year. I wanted him to start in August, but he said he wasn't ready to start so soon. He wanted to do a little traveling and see the world before being bogged down with school work. I completely understood where he came from. At the beginning of September, I surprised him, Myia, and Jy'Lon with a two-week vacation to Dubai. Then, we went out west to check on my rental properties for four days. While we were out there, there wasn't a way we were going to pass up going to Las Vegas. Next, we hit up Orlando for seven days. The only reason we didn't stay longer was because I wanted to sit down and chat with Marlon. I told Trandall and Myia that they needed to talk to him as well.

The visit went well; it was very emotional, to the point that Trandall walked off after saying what he had to say to his cousin; a close cousin who he had forgiven but didn't see the same anymore. Myia spoke to her brother in the same manner as Trandall—straight to the point. She laid his ass out in a way that I had to cut in and tell her to chill. She left the same way she came in—not fazed at all. I was the last one to speak to him. I sincerely forgave him. When I stood up, he had tears streaming down his face. After all that we had been through, I couldn't turn my back on him, so I informed him that I would send him pictures of the babies, Marlia, and the rest of our family. He didn't need to know that from time-to-time I would put money on his books.

That would be Zy'Lon's and my little secret; yes, I informed my fiancée of what I wanted to do with some of the money that Charles left me.

Before I left the jail, there wasn't anything else that I could say; thus, I just stared at Marlon. The little boy who had a severe crush on me, had the pleasure of having me in his bed, and in his arms was facing some serious jail time for his malicious acts.

I had to shake my head as I finally found the will to walk away. He banged on the table as he called my name and said that he was sorry. I had tears streaming down my face as I would never see that little boy prosper the way that he should have. I would never see that little boy be the father that he was supposed to be to Marlia. She would spend her time with Myia, Momma Linda, Grandma Sylvia, and me. We were her guardians nowall because her father decided to do some shit he had no business doing.

Grandma Sylvia cut ties with Marlon the moment she got wind of him being the reason for the shooting at my grandmother's house. She never forgave him, talked, or visited him. She acted as if he never existed, and I hate to say it, but that shit tore me up inside. I tried talking to her, but she was hell bent on how she felt about her irresponsible, careless grandson. Just like Myia and Trandall, Momma Linda was on the fence with her son. I highly believed if it wasn't for Marlia, she wouldn't have dealt with him either.

Trandall left out two weeks ago with his girlfriend turned fiancée Vanessa. She had joined the military, and he thought it was best to be in the same state as her while she completed basic training. In actuality, he was leaving the state of Alabama because he didn't want to be near Marlon even though he was beyond bars. I wished him much luck and success in everything that he and Vanessa did. Like the big sister that I was to them when we were younger, I made sure to send him off with a nice rubber-banded stack of money. He tried to refuse, but I wasn't hearing that shit.

Our lives were forever changed because of Marlon, but parts of it were good changes. Jy'Lon, Zy'Lon, and Trandall left the streets behind. Myia found real happiness with Jy'Lon, and just like me, she was engaged as well. Thanks to Vincent, my mother had been enjoying life instead of sulking about the things my father put me through and the death of her mother. She was happy and smiling more.

We took the good with the bad and made the best out of it. That's what I preached to Momma Linda and Grandma Sylvia every time I talked to them, but they didn't see things that way. They were hell bent on not accepting what Marlon had done. All I could do was pray on that front.

"Cannon-motherfuckin'-ball!" Jy'Lon yelled as he jumped off the diving board, brining me to reality.

Laughing, I shook my head at that foolish man who was really a big kid at heart.

"Look at his yella ass. He gonna be complainin' tonight about being sunburned. I don't want to hear a bitch ass word about his body hurting when I molest his ass tonight," Myia voiced before laughing.

As I giggled at her comment, Zy'Lon surfaced from underneath the pool's cool, refreshing, water and said, "Bring yo' gorgeous, pregnant ass here, Sexy Chocolate."

With a smile on my face, I stood and pranced over to my man. Helping me into the pool, he sexily groaned, causing me to coo. I loved the noises that came out of his mouth. That shit turned me the fuck on.

As he secured me around his waist, he moved us towards the other end of the pool. Loving the sight of us, I quickly shoved my head towards his. With care and precision, I sucked on his lips before sticking my tongue in his mouth. His right hand found its way towards my white and green polka dotted swimming bottoms, and I gave him full-access to toy with my hungry pussy.

"Issa fuckin' session in the pool! Myia bring yo' ass here, guh!" Jy'Lon yelled excitedly.

"You know damn well I can't swim, Jy'Lon," Myia replied, laughing.

"This dick will keep yo' ass afloat. Nih, get yo' ass to me now!" he loudly replied, causing us to laugh.

The moment Myia was secured around Jy'Lon's waist, we screamed, "Issa fuckin' session in the pool!"

Turning his head to me, Zy'Lon seriously looked at me and said, "I'm goin' to enjoy being yo' husband, yo' partner, yo' lover man, an' the father of our child an' future kids fo' the rest of my life."

"And, I'm going to enjoy being your wife, your dirty little freak, the mother to your child and future children, and your partner for life. I love you, Zy'Lon Ronan Greggory."

"I love you, Sasha Nicole Pierce ... fuck that, Sasha Nicole Greggory."

Chuckling, I said, "You better get that shit right."

"To us!" Jy'Lon happily yelled from afar.

"To us!" we replied before engaging in the sexual fun.

About the Author

TN Jones resides in the state of Alabama with her daughter. Growing up, TN Jones always had a passion for and writing, which led her to writing short stories.

In 2015, TN Jones began working on her first book, *Disloyal: Revenge of a Broken Heart*, which was previously titled, *Passionate Betrayals*.

TN Jones writes in the following genres: Women's Fiction, Mystery/Suspense, Urban Fiction/Romance, Dark Erotica/Erotica, and Urban/Interracial Paranormal.

Published novels by TN Jones: *Disloyal: Revenge of a Broken Heart, Disloyal 2-3: A Woman's Revenge, A Sucka in Love for a Thug, If You'll Give Me Your Heart 1-2, By Any Means: Going Against the Grain 1-2, The Sins of Love: Finessing the Enemies 1-3, Caught Up In a D-Boy's Illest Love 1-3, Choosing To Love A*

Lady Thug 1-4, Is This Your Man, Sis: Side Piece Chronicles, Just You and Me: A Magical Love Story, and *Jonesin' For A Boss Chick: A Montgomery Love Story.*

Upcoming novels by TN Jones*: You Ain't Gotta Say Too Much* and many more.

Thank you for reading the finale of *That Young Hood Love*. Leave an honest review under the book title on Amazon.

For future book details, please visit any of the links below:

Amazon Author page:

https://www.amazon.com/tnjones666

Facebook:

https://www.facebook.com/novelisttnjones/

Goodreads:

https://www.goodreads.com/author/show/14918893. TN_Jones:

Google+:

https://www.plus.google.com/u/1/communities/11505 7649956960897339

Instagram:

https://www.instagram.com/tnjones666

Twitter: https://twitter.com/TNHarris6.

You are welcome to *email* her:

tnjones666@gmail.com

Chat with her daily in the Facebook groups: *Its Just Me...TN Jones* and *Sipping and Chilling with Tyanna Presents.*

CPSIA information can be obtained
at www.ICGtesting.com
Printed in the USA
LVHW012148070120
642793LV00005B/688

9 781070 397818